girl on
a float

D0998855

girl on a float

BY BRIAN BEDARD

North Dakota State University Press
NDSU Dept. 2360, P.O. Box 6050
Fargo, ND 58108-6050
www.ndsupress.org

North Dakota State University Press
NDSU Dept. 2360, P.O. Box 6050
Fargo, ND 58108-6050
www.ndsupress.org

GIRL ON A FLOAT
By Brian Bedard

Copyright © 2020 North Dakota State University Press
All rights reserved. This book may not be reproduced in whole or part in any
form without permission from the publisher. For copyright permission, contact
Suzanne Kelley at 701-231-6848 or suzanne.kelley@ndsu.edu

First Edition
First Printing

The publication of *Girl on a Float* is made possible by the generous support of
donors to the NDSU Press Fund and the NDSU Press Endowment Fund, and
other contributors to NDSU Press.

David Bertolini, Director
Suzanne Kelley, Publisher
Zachary Vietz, Graduate Assistant in Publishing
Taylor Flakker, Publishing Intern

Jamie Hohnadel Trosen, Cover Designer
Deb Tanner, Interior Designer

International Standard Book Number: 978-1-946163-14-1
Library of Congress Control Number: 2019954568

Printed in the United States of America

Publisher's Cataloging-In-Publication Data
(Prepared by The Donohue Group, Inc.)

Names: Bedard, Brian, 1945- author.
Title: Girl on a float / by Brian Bedard.
Description: First edition. | Fargo, ND : North Dakota State University
    Press, [2020]
Identifiers: ISBN 9781946163141
Subjects: LCSH: Country life--Great Plains--Fiction. | Farm life--Great
    Plains--Fiction. | Families--Great Plains--Fiction. | Family farms--
    Great Plains--Fiction. | LCGFT: Short stories. | BISAC: FICTION / Short
    Stories (single author) | FICTION / Literary. | FICTION / Small Town &
    Rural.
Classification: LCC PS3552.E287 G57 2020 | DDC 813/.54--dc23

This is a work of fiction. Names, characters, businesses, places, events, locales, and
incidents are either the products of the author's imagination or used in a fictitious
manner. Any resemblance to actual persons, living or dead, or actual events is
purely coincidental.

For Sharon,
Artist of the heart, keeper of the spirit.

contents

part i:
the elements

Bright clear sky over a plain so wide that the rim of the heavens cut down on it around the entire horizon . . . bright, clear sky, to-day, tomorrow, and for all time to come.
    . . . And sun! And still more sun! It set the heavens afire every morning; it grew with the day to quivering golden light—then softened into all the shades of red and purple as evening fell . . . Pure color everywhere. A gust of wind, sweeping across the plain, threw into life waves of yellow and blue and green. Now and then a dead black wave would race across the scene . . . a cloud's gliding shadow . . . now and then.

                      —O. E. Rolvaag, *Giants in the Earth*

All things in the plain are isolate; there is no confusion of objects in the eye, but *one* hill or *one* tree or *one* man. At the slightest elevation you can see to the end of the world. To look upon that landscape in the early morning, with the sun at your back, is to lose the sense of proportion. Your imagination comes to life, and this, you think, is where Creation was begun.

                    —N. Scott Momaday, *House Made of Dawn*

Meltdown

FIRST, THERE WAS A GOLD and white flash from the cornstalks twenty feet from the reservation road, then a burst of rust and black feathers, and then a startling apparition veering toward the windshield. The scarlet hood, the startled black eye, the white ring on the pheasant's neck loomed in a startling close-up before it slammed into the glass, blood fanning in streaks as the pheasant rolled away. Leslie Hendricks made the mistake of tracking on it, craning her neck to see where it had gone. In seconds she lost control of the Schwenk's delivery truck, her foot still holding the gas pedal down as the truck veered off the shoulder of the road and plunged into a ditch. Leslie jolted in panic at the sight of a massive pine tree rising from the ditch into the prairie's wide blue horizon. She hit the brake at the last second but was only able to slow the truck to 25 before slamming into the tree.

The impact snapped her back and neck, then pitched her forward, the seatbelt locking just as her head collided with the windshield and pulling her back into place behind the wheel. She stared, stunned, at the pine branches spread across the windshield, curled around the rearview mirror, could see steam snaking through the dark needles. She lightly touched a cut oozing blood below the hairline on her forehead, then wiped her fingertips on her jeans and checked herself for other cuts or signs of broken bones. She was still in one piece and was not seriously injured. The engine had died, so she pulled the keys out of the ignition before prying the door open and climbing out.

The front of the truck was bent around the tree trunk, the grill and hood caved in and angled toward the ground. Water and oil were running out of gaps and splits in the truck's hood. In the warm, wide quiet of the August morning, she could hear the compressor on the refrigerator unit sputtering, screeching until, with a sudden popping sound, it died.

Leslie glanced at her watch, its face burning with the glare of a hot summer day. Ten twenty-three, and it was already sweltering. She hurried around to the trailer to see if the auxiliary generator had kicked in.

Down on her knees in the tall, dusty grass, she saw that the generator was caved in and flattened. A few drops of moisture were already dripping through a split in its bottom and from the drain plugs spaced along the bottom of the trailer. Watching the drops stretch, flicker, and vanish into the earth, she felt as though her hopes and plans were disappearing with them.

Securing the Royal River Casino account was going to be her way of meeting her sales quotas, surpassing her monthly minimums, and earning enough extra money for a down payment on a small house. Which meant that she wouldn't have to keep listening to the couple in the apartment above hers strain the bedsprings while grunting and moaning their way through the weekend. Listening to their noises was almost as bad as listening to Dutch, the district supervisor, harp at her about increasing sales, creating new markets, filing more detailed reports, building relationships, increasing sales, attending leadership seminars in Kansas City, increasing sales. And then pulling her out of the eastern Nebraska district just when she was beginning to develop a profitable route and assigning her to eastern South Dakota, telling her that the small farm towns and the reservations were an untapped gold mine. Gold was Dutch's favorite word—golden opportunity, gold at the end of the rainbow, going for gold. It all matched the gold crowns on his teeth and the gold necklaces that flashed from the open necks of his Hawaiian shirts.

The only gold she'd seen out on the South Dakota prairie shone across vast stretches of corn stubble in morning light, which she didn't dare look at for too long or she'd fall asleep at the wheel. The other gold she kind of liked—the throbbing gold petals of sunflowers lifting their faces to the sky in a field of black-centered faces. But both the cornfields and the sunflowers were actually just patches of color she passed, objects in a world she had no connection with, a world that meant only large patches of dirt and weeds and stands of wind-blistered trees scattered between the delivery points on her route.

Even in the towns she saw no sign of things familiar and exciting—just a recurring ensemble of cinderblock bars, tawdry little grocery stores with dirty windows and old-fashioned signs, mismatched facades on the downtown buildings, and grain elevators or car lots coming in or going out. The people she bought meals, gas, or cold drinks from were pleasant and polite enough, but listening to their conversations in cafes and convenience stores, it was clear that their horizons ended at the edge of town. Nice people, kind people, but no real edge to them. She was used to dealing with city people and city pace, and she wasn't sure if she would ever be able to feel she belonged out here in all this harsh weather and mind-boggling space.

The only thing that had kept her going so far were the private sales goals she had set for herself—a numbers game that put some tension and adventure in her days. Which was why she was eager to get the Royal River Casino account. Also because, of all the contact points she'd encountered in South Dakota, she'd felt most at home in the casinos. They had just

enough of the old flavor of recklessness and impulse and escape she'd known in her Kansas City drinking, gambling, and
dancing haunts, which she knew weren't the best places for
her and often got her into debt and or danger of some kind,
but which also helped her break the monotony of her job selling frozen food from a truck. Here there seemed to be no such
release for her.

She'd heard a long time ago that this was how the company kept people from getting too many years in and building up
retirement. Just wait until someone had twelve or fifteen years
in, then start screwing with their routes, their schedule, ratch-
et up their goals, needle them with vague threats. In short,
encourage them to quit. It was hard for her to tell if this was
happening or not. She kept it all out of her head as much as
possible, found ways to meet her goals and keep her mouth
shut. But it was starting to take its toll on her. She had begun
to think more and more about returning to U of Nebraska,
Omaha, and finishing her computer science degree, which she
had abandoned when rising costs finally overwhelmed her.
This job paid the bills and gave her a chance to travel and meet
people, and, for a while, it had seemed like she was advanc-
ing. But now the whole transfer thing was beginning to seem
like a set-up Dutch had come up with: assign her an untested,
poverty-stricken route, give her the truck with the worst re-
frigeration unit in the entire fleet, and then ride her for not
meeting quotas some bean counter had dreamed up while
running a fever.

She felt suddenly like she was running a fever and realized
she'd better get out of the sun. She spotted a patch of shade on
the far side of the tree she'd run into, walked over to it, and
sat down. It crossed her mind suddenly to call Dutch on her
cell phone, tell him the news. She reached for the cell phone

cradled in a holster on her hip but didn't lift it out. She could already hear his voice sliding into overdrive and peppering her with incriminating questions. She could sense she might just start screaming or cursing uncontrollably. She didn't dare cut loose on him; there was too much at stake. Nine years of her life were tied up in the smashed hood and melting cargo of the ruined red truck sitting in front of her.

She took a deep breath, then lay down in the grass and looked up at the sky. It arched away in a dome of tepid air, and for a moment she was lost in the sweep of it. She watched as a flock of tiny black birds, thick as a congregation of gnats, expanded and contracted into different shapes as it crossed the sky. She could hear the chirping and squawking of other birds in the cornstalks to her left, but she couldn't see any birds. Red-winged grasshoppers leaped on her chest and whirred away in soft clatters, making her almost forget where she was.

Human voices stirred her into focus, and she sat up to see two people coming toward her on the narrow, weed-crowded road, carrying something in their arms. They were almost to her when she saw that they were carrying bags of groceries and that they were Lakota Indians, a woman who appeared in her mid-fifties, wearing denim dungarees and a turquoise t-shirt, and an elderly man in khaki pants, white Coca-Cola t-shirt, and red cap. They waved to her as though greeting an old friend, and she stopped wondering where they had gotten groceries in this ocean of cornfields and dead-end roads, and began wondering if they thought that she was someone else.

They kept the same slow pace even though they could see the wrecked truck and her standing beside it.

"Hey," the woman called. "Looks like you had a little problem with that tree."

"How's your head?" the old man added, eyeing the sun-blackened gash on Leslie's forehead.

"I'm OK," Leslie said. "The truck's in pretty bad shape, though."

"Sorry to hear that," the woman said, her long, straight hair blowing in columns of blue-black sheen.

Up close, she looked younger. She had a smooth, attractive face and provocative eyes. The old man, both arms wrapped around the IGA letters on his grocery bag, was more drawn in the face than he'd appeared at a distance, but his white hair, woven into a single braid, had a thickness and fullness that startled her, and his eyes were dark and piercing, but not unfriendly.

"This here's Thelma Mireau," he said. "I'm Desmond Smokes Pipe."

"Pleased to meet you. I'm Leslie Hendricks. I had a pheasant hit my windshield, and I quit paying attention to my driving."

"Them pheasant'll do it," the old man said. "Deer, too. Jump right on your hood."

"Does your truck still run?" the woman said.

"It's shot. It's leaking every kind of fluid it has in it."

"Wasn't your fault," the woman said. "Things like pheasants and deer, they just happen out here. They can happen to anyone."

Leslie could feel tears welling up.

"It was my fault," she said. "I wasn't paying attention to what I was doing, and now I've wrecked the damn truck, and I won't get the Royal River account, and they'll take away my route and stick me in the warehouse, and . . ."

"Hold on, hold on," the woman said. "It's just an old truck and a bunch of TV dinners."

"Yeah," the old man said. "Most of that stuff ain't even food."

The woman smiled, shook her head, and looked at Leslie.

"Desmond traps or fishes for most of his food," she said.

"You betcha," the old man said. "Squirrel stew. That's what a man should eat if he wants to live long. I got some potatoes, tomatoes, and carrots in this bag for fixing it tonight."

Leslie nodded at his strong resolve.

"But you don't understand," she said. "It's all down the drain. Everything I've worked for."

"How old are you?" the woman said, shifting the weight of her grocery bags as she studied the narrow strip of highway where it curved and disappeared in the corn.

"Twenty-nine."

The woman smiled, her dark eyes holding Leslie in their tranquil gaze.

"You're just a kid," she said.

She turned to the old man.

"Maybe we can get her a wrecker out here from Mission Hill, Desmond. We have to walk over that way."

"Marvin's gone walleye fishing," the old man said. "Ain't anyone in Mission Hill can drive that wrecker but him."

"I appreciate your concern," Leslie said. "But I'll be OK. Is there a highway patrol office near here?"

"That's way up to Sisseton," the old man said. "Other side of Royal River."

"Royal River is where I'm supposed to deliver most of this stuff," Leslie said. "Almost everything on the truck is theirs except for a few home orders in Flandreau."

The old man grinned, and she saw that he had only four teeth, two on the top and two on the bottom.

"Royal River is gonna lose that bet," he said. "Nobody's gonna win a bet with the sun."

"It looks that way," Leslie said. "But could you maybe stop at a sheriff's office or police station and see if someone could come out and help?"

"We'll do our best," the woman said.

"Thanks for stopping," Leslie said. "And nice meeting you."

She watched them walk away in the heat, blending with the haze they had come out of. She made an awning over her eyes with her hand, glanced at the sun in its high, burning locus, and walked around the truck to sit in the shade and think things out. She'd wait half an hour, max, then walk across the fields in the direction of the freeway. Or else she would start walking toward Flandreau, hoping someone would pick her up along the way. She started thinking of ways to explain to Dutch what had happened, how to word it. But it was far too hot to think, so she crawled under the truck to take another look at the damage while she was waiting for Thelma and Desmond to send help.

When she crawled back out fifteen minutes later, she saw several Lakota children peering at her around the rear corner of the truck. A few were barefoot, some wore flip flops or tennis shoes without socks, and their clothing was faded from summer sun and frequent washings. A few wore baseball caps. One had a straw cowboy hat much too big for his head. Leslie stood up, brushed herself off, and straightened her clothing. When she reached the group gathered near the rear of the truck, she said, "Pretty hot today, isn't it?"

Most of the children just stared at her. A boy of nine or ten, wearing a LeBron James jersey and a pair of silky black trunks that spilled over his knees, stepped closer. He had a beaded coin purse tied around his wrist.

"Is your stuff all melted?"

"Not yet," Leslie said. "But it's getting there."

"Can we buy some?" a little girl in a plaid jumpsuit said. "You got any Bomb Pops or Dilly Bars?"

Leslie laughed.

"Yes, I do. But I couldn't charge you for them. They're half melted."

"We don't care," the little girl said. "If they're still cold."

"Wait right here," Leslie said.

In this way, the distribution began. A few of the children stayed for a second and third fudge stick or Bomb Pop. The others scattered into the fields, slipped into the corn, scurried down the road on their bicycles.

Before long, more children arrived, a few Lakota boys on three wheelers bouncing out of the ditches to skid in the dust and kill their engines. The boy in the James jersey helped Leslie pass out novelties until they were almost all gone, then they dipped into the softening pizzas, cinnamon rolls, pies, coffee cakes, and cylinders of Häagen-Dazs ice cream. The boy in the jersey took delight in reading the flavors off as he tossed them to a group of his junior high friends, who had ridden over on horseback to join the celebration.

"Hey! You got any of those Nestle Crunch Bars?" one of them said.

"No," Leslie said. "But how about some low fat sundae cups?"

"Take 'em, Delbert," a teenage girl in a two-piece said. "Give your horse a break."

They all laughed and chided the boy on the tired-looking mare.

"Let's have the sundae cups," he said.

Before long, several adult Lakota arrived, some looking at the merchandise in the rear of the truck, some walking around the front to survey the damage. An old woman in a checkered cotton dress and black shawl was pushing a wheelbarrow. She was able to get most of the chicken teriyaki meal kits in the wheelbarrow, which she guided onto a cow path that skirted the corn in the direction of some distant bluffs. A man, who introduced himself as Melvin Sleeping Bear, told Leslie he had room in his freezer for the frozen fish. He stood for several minutes in the shade of the truck, pondering the glossy photos of exotic ocean fish with labels such as Breaded Blue Hake, New England Scrod, Alaskan Stuffed Monterrey Sole, and Lobster Au Gratin.

"Them's good pictures," he said. "After I eat the fish, I can hang them pictures on my walls."

Then he slid most of them under a tarp in the bed of his badly oxidized El Camino and pulled away.

Leslie was so caught up in emptying the truck that she lost track of time until it was almost three o'clock. When she asked the group present at the time if anyone had contacted the sheriff, they all looked at her with blank expressions. A Lakota man in his early twenties, who had just arrived on a motorcycle, waved her over to where he sat spit-cleaning a Marilyn Monroe tattoo on his right bicep.

"What is it?" Leslie said.

"When you get that thing emptied, I can give you a ride over to Flandreau."

She paused, glanced at the defunct truck and then at the gleaming motorcycle.

"I've never ridden on a motorcycle," she said.

"Then you got a chance to start livin'," the young man said.

"But I don't even know you."

"I'm Lester Mireau. My sister, Thelma, sent me to help you."

"Thelma? Oh, Thelma. All right then. I should be ready in about twenty minutes."

When she had given away the last three boxes, she closed the metal doors and locked the cab of the truck. Then she climbed on the back of the motorcycle, and they roared off,

Leslie's arms clamped tight around the young man's waist, her hair billowing in the wind.

Traveling this way, she felt the sting of insects glancing off her arms and face, sensed her spirit boring like a frenzied worm into the deep recesses of the green and yellow fields. The radiant geometry of sunflowers baring their broad faces to the sun, the lift of a pale brown hawk from a rotting post, the flaming surfaces of stock ponds and sloughs, the dense green jungles of ditches where pheasants lurked, cattails trembling in the shimmer of heat. The singe of a scorching wind burned the detritus of city from the edges of her heart.

They were traveling at break-neck speed, but she felt no fear, felt only the hard, muscular body of the driver as he gunned the cycle like a rocket launched from Hell. In the bellowing rush of wind, in the scorching leer of the sun, she lost her troubled aims and entered the plains.

Coyote Bait

FROM THE BUNK IN HER room just off the kitchen the little girl could see pieces of her parents moving, could hear talking in the kitchen on a sweltering August night. At first she couldn't tell what they were talking about, and then she saw the cat's tail twitching, curling around one of her father's knees.

"I haven't had any luck hunting the bastards, so I'm going to try Grandpa's method."

"I don't like the sound of it," her mother said.

"Nothing to it," her father said. "Just tie the cat to that post near the barn, then go sit in the dark, and wait."

"You mean you're going to leave him out there by himself so those coyotes can just come in and kill him?"

The little girl tensed in her bed, her eyes wide, watching the cat's spotted tail, her heart pounding with the realization of which cat this was.

"There won't be anybody killed but the coyotes," her father was saying. "Butch here will be on top of the post by the time the shooting starts."

"That's awful," her mother said. "It's cruel. And you'll scare Martha out of her wits."

"Nothing cruel about it. Grandpa did it for years. Never lost a cat. And the noise will glance off Martha like a thunderstorm passing in the night."

He swung around, and Martha could see one of the cat's eyes, a slice of its tail through the crack in the door.

"The thing to remember is that this is a barn cat, June. He knows how to take care of himself."

"You could sit up all night waiting."

"When Butch gets through making a fuss about being tied up, a whole family of coyotes will be sitting out there by the barn, trying to decide who goes first."

"I can't believe they'd be so dumb as to come right into the yard."

"I ain't arguing about them being smart. But they got a weakness. They like to eat cats."

"Don't I know it. That's probably what happened to Mickey and Max."

Martha frowned, pulled harder on the daisy appliqué she was peeling off her pajama top. They had told her the cats ran away. For a moment she was sickened by the thought of the coyotes dragging her cats into the wheat and eating them. Then she heard her mother closing cupboards and drawers, heard her father's boots on the linoleum as he moved toward the back porch. The kitchen light went off, and the house darkened. She climbed off the bunk, crossed the room, and parted the curtains to peer out at the back lot. She watched her father carry the cat out to the post in the silver white glare of the yard light.

Once the cat was secured, her father melded with the blackness. The cat remained, hunched on the ground, tail twitching in the dust. When the cat began to yowl, Martha pulled the curtains shut and hurried over to her bed.

She tried to close the yowling out, fixing her eyes on the tinfoil star she had made in school last Christmas. She thought of sleeping out on the porch where she could see the sky and the millions of blinking stars on quiet summer nights. She tried to remember the names of the constellations, but could only think of Big Dipper. She changed the picture in her head, saw the big calico the first time she had coaxed him out from under the porch of the hired man's house. He came slowly into the sunlight as he nosed toward the fish head she had tied to a long piece of rope.

She had lured him into the tool shed, and then quickly closed the door. He didn't resist the doll clothes she had put on him, except for the bonnet, which he kept swiping at with his front paws. It was her favorite bonnet from her best doll, and she had hesitated using it, but it was the only one big enough to fit a cat's head. While she was taking the other clothes off him later that afternoon, he had bolted away with the bonnet still on his head and had torn it off somewhere in the fields. She'd been angry with him for a long time, but thinking about it now and hearing him yowling, she wasn't angry anymore.

She turned over, closed her eyes, and tried to count sheep the way her grandmother Lewis had taught her. She counted as far as twenty-three when the air rocked with a rifle shot, then a second, and a third.

She was at the window in a flash, ears ringing as she scanned the brightly-lit yard. She saw her father down on one knee, rolling two dead coyotes over, bloodspots spreading on their bellies and necks. The cat, scrunched into a ball at the top of the post, was watching silently as Martha's father dragged the coyotes over to his pick-up and tossed them into the bed. Then he walked back to the post and lifted the cat down.

Martha's pulse was slowing down; she thought he would let the cat loose now. Instead, he carried it into the house. The kitchen light came on, and she heard the refrigerator opening. Her father passed through the slit, carrying the cat and a bowl. The screen door slapped.

When her father came back in, turned the kitchen light out, and clomped up the stairs to his room, Martha got down from the bunk and opened her door, entering the dim kitchen. She crossed to the screen door and paused to peer out. At first, she couldn't see the cat, but then she saw it crouched over the bowl of milk. In the heat-swollen quietness of the night, she could hear the rapid little licking sound around which the fields of wheat and the star-crowded sky seemed to hover.

Appendix to the Air King
Cell Phone Owner's Manual

AIR KING CELL PHONE STANDS behind the guarantees and warranties contained in this pamphlet, but we strongly suggest that, before using your new cell phone, you read two history books on the 1880s in South Dakota. (See page 5 for additional recommended readings.) These books will sharpen your sense of local terrain and weather. They will chasten you with a harsh reminder of wind on the Northern Plains. They will illustrate the kind of human spirit South Dakotans are famous for and will crystallize conditions in which your forebears experienced winter, compared with the ways you ward it off in the early twenty-first century. Your new cell phone is one major contrast, along with your four-wheel drive SUV, your all-season tires, your polar fleece, your Lennox furnace, your double-pane windows, and your Sorel boots.

As the history books will tell you, you are facing a terrain that has been exposed to wind, snow, and ice storms for at least six hundred million years. A terrain that was once completely covered with ice, then completely covered with water. Then inhabited by dinosaurs, giant sloths, saber-toothed tigers, and other pre-historic beasts, all of whom vanished, along with the primitive mound builders, who came after them, and by the Indian tribes who came after them, and the nineteenth-century pioneers who came after them. We don't have much record of all the waves that bleeped across the computer screen of those eras like so many whirling flakes in an endless blizzard. Or like the waves of grasshoppers who raided the Northern

Plains in the 1870s—wide, undulating clouds of Rocky Mountain locusts, darkening the sky as they swept over South Dakota in the summers of 1873, '74, and '75, and fell on the open land like rain showers on fields of ripening grain.

Settlers took the grasshopper plagues in stride. They eked out a living until they could recover their crops, then looked nervously at the horizon to see nothing but prairie rolling green and yellow into an unblemished sky for the next three years. Be sure to read also the section on the hard winter of 1880–81, which followed the plagues, having waited almost demonically for the settlers to recover their crops and their hopes for their journey into the 1880s. Take careful note of the blizzard that hit the plains in mid-October of 1880.

It surprised both Lakota Indians and white settlers, who were shocked by the depths of snow but thought that the freak timing would be righted by mild, snow-melting temperatures in November before more snow arrived. Imagine their surprise when the snow didn't melt, when successive snowfalls added layer upon layer to an already snow-buried ground and covered the state from one end to the other. Imagine hundreds of settlers caught off guard without provisions or shelter. Imagine trainloads of fuel stranded and buried on railroad sidings for the next four months. In their frenzy to ward off the cold, settlers burned twisted hay, straw, and ear-corn. Town dwellers cut up small buildings, fences, bridges, and piles of new lumber. Oil for lamps was in short supply, as were candles, tallow, and lard. Snow covering the roofs of both log cabins and sod houses deepened the darkness.

Outside, thousands of cattle froze. Some were gathered in crude barns and fed through holes in the roof. When forage ran out, the cattle starved or froze to death. Meanwhile, the settlers, groping around darkened houses the size of a modern one-car garage, created a food supply by grinding small amounts of wheat in coffee mills. Cut off from the outside world, they waited in darkness while snowplows and shoveling crews struggled to clear the tracks of drifts the height of three boxcars.

Settlers hunkered down, their days and nights passing as slowly as the growth of icicles on their roofs. On into December and January, boosting their spirits with dreams of spring. By early February their nerves were frayed, their spirits sagging when yet another blizzard swept cross the plains. From there to March, they bore more cold and cloud cover, taking their only real pleasure in a February thaw that softened the surface of the drifts, then froze, forming an impenetrable crust. During this brief hiatus, they ventured to partake in the best sledding they'd ever had. They turned winter back on itself, later writing in their journals that they never enjoyed a winter more than the winter of the big blockade.

The thaw rejuvenated them long enough to face the flood of 1881, which broke loose in late March and for which nothing could have braced them. They'd been waiting since October for a break in the weather. By mid-March the break came when snowmelt in the upper country sent water down over the lower, ice-choked channels of the Big Sioux, the James, and the Missouri Rivers. On the twentieth of March, 1881, the Big Sioux River rose sixteen feet above its low-water mark in twenty-four hours. Torrents knocked out five bridges in fifteen minutes, covering the bottomland west of Sioux Falls with ten feet of water. Farmers in the bottoms plunged from being owners of small fortunes in grain and livestock to being paupers overnight. From the highlands, people watched buildings float past, saw barns and houses flooded to their rooftops. Homesteads on the James River vanished under water when the James rose twenty feet near Huron, washed away the courthouse at Forestberg, and wrecked large numbers of clay homes belonging to German-Russian immigrants.

At Yankton, the Missouri finished the disaster. Lowlands flooded at Pierre from backed-up water. Oxen used on freight routes to Deadwood were swept downstream and drowned. The White Swan settlement near Fort Randall followed the oxen.

Listen to these names: Austin, Bliss, Brookings, Christopherson, Deuel, Ewing, Fitch, Gregory, Hanson, Jayne, Jolley, Madsen, Manning, Mickelson, Merrigan, O'Gorman, Phelps, Picotte, Pinney, Rasmussen, Stewart, Walker, Zitterkopf. These are the old Dakota Territory names, names now indelible in the history of the state. They lack the poetry of the famous Lakota names—Sitting Bull, Crazy Horse— but they are the wanderers who clawed with hoes the lunar distance you now leap across with cell phones, slicing through air gray with whispers from their graves.

On an eerie Sunday morning in late March, throngs of people gathered on the riverbank at Yankton, eyeing the wintering fleet of steamboats when the ice jam broke and gave way, pinching the steamer, the *Western*, against the bank and crushing it before the river cleared. The crowd was terrified but relieved that the river was clear. They didn't know that the ice had broken earlier in the upper end of the river near Springfield. With ice not yet melted in the lower river below Yankton, water had backed up and flooded the lowlands, submerging the James River bottom.

Then came the killer break. Just before noon at midweek, settlers felt and heard an immense shudder run through the gorge. As *The Dakota Herald* described it, "Water gave a mighty roar and with a sudden jerk the whole tremendous mass began to rear and crash and tumble, as if it knew of its awful power of destruction." Icebergs smashed steamboats along the river's edge, lifted them out of the river, and dumped them on the bank in pieces. Only because of a levee of ice on the riverfront was a major portion of Yankton spared. Vermillion, twenty-three miles downstream, was not as fortunate. The Missouri poured into it, demolishing the town and driving residents to the bluffs above the town.

Ten people died in the flood of 1881, which lasted close to a week. Beyond the human deaths, thousands of animals and birds lay dead in the muck. The stench of their decay hung in the air as a haunting reminder of snow falling hard in a distant October. Imprinted in the hearts and minds of your ancestors were the images and sensations of a lifetime. Winter's worst scenes were etched in permanent recollection, just as they were etched in the memory of a Lakota named Strike-the-Ree, who dictated a letter to a newspaper editor in Yankton on April 5, 1881, that stated, "It is now some eighty winters that I have seen the snow fall and melt away along this Missouri River, but I never saw a winter of such snow and floods as these . . . Long ago—forty years or more—there was a flood that overtook and killed a large number of Teton Sioux, but even then the flood was not as high as this."

The influx of settlers into Dakota Territory in the late spring of 1881 did not slow. It surged on, sparked by the revival of snow-soaked dirt. The settlers dug into summer, into an autumn of good crops, into an extremely mild winter in which farming went on every month, and little snow fell. These were your ancestors pressing forward, hacking out a life, enduring the winters of 1886 and '87. These were the bearers of children who died in the blizzard of 1888, which Edwin C. Torrey described in *Early Days in Dakota 1907* as "the fiercest, maddest cyclone or hurricane of snow that ever assaulted the middle west."

The Saga of
Webster World Turner

HOW HE GOT OUT, YOU know, was he was in between them two other guys, and they kept him warm. That, and the pint of Irish Rose wine he had inside his coat, which he took nips on once the other two stopped talking and started dozing off. But not Webster. Webster stayed warm, crawled back into the hole of himself, just like a badger, you know, and when a badger goes into his hole to stay, you can't get him out except with dynamite.

So there you have old Webster out on the road between Fort Thompson and Pukwana with his two pals, and he's dreaming, you know, he's riding the range of his dreams. It's a big range, we can tell you that, because he's told us some of them stories before, and he's got a big range of dreams to feed on. Food for the spirit, as any Lakota knows. It will last for a long time since it don't have nothing to do with time the way the white man thinks about time with clocks and watches and all that stuff they call timepieces. Webster had timepieces, all right, but not nothing like you can buy at J. C. Penney's. He had a whole medicine bag full of timepieces, and he just went into his head and dragged them out one at a time and turned them over in the light.

They made him feel so damn good inside it warmed his blood even when the men on either side of him were freezing to death.

It's because Webster knew his people, the history of the Lakota people. He knew all those stories and songs, just like holding a leather pouch with little owl feathers and rabbit feet and elk teeth in it. Finding that warmth and holding onto it was just like sitting in a sweat lodge with Tobias Young Bear, the medicine man who raised him. He could see the plains in summer and the buffalo herds and the young men mingling with the herd, coaxing it toward the jumps, spooking it into a thundering run. He could hear the hooves pounding on the roof of that Ford Falcon—a thousand stampeding buffalo plunging off the roof of his car down a shale cliff. Breaking on the rocks, bleeding from their mouths, and then bunches of sage and little stands of chokecherries turning into women with skinning knives. Slitting their throats to end all the twitching and bawling, and Webster watched the blood seep into the burning dust.

Webster felt the heat rising from the slaughter, saw the blood-streaked beads of skinners swinging in the sun. Just the sight of it was enough to keep his heart pumping he told us down at the Broken Arrow Inn his first day back. He could hear his heart beating like a drum he remembered hearing before he was born.

That's how Webster was spending the night while we were all out searching for him in the snow and wind once we got word that he and Dan and Howard decided to chance driving over to Fort Thompson from Marty. He told us how they hit a drift about ten miles down the road and couldn't go nowhere or see nothing, so they all climbed into the back seat to try to keep each other warm until someone could come and rescue them. They had a little argument at first about staying put, with Howard wanting to get out and start walking. Howard was thinking he could find the way back to Fort Thompson. Said he'd been in a blizzard before, so he opens the door to get out, and Webster grabs his coat to pull him back in. Told him, "You ain't going anywhere, you crazy Indian." Howard tugged and slapped at Webster and tried to bite Webster's hand. But Webster won out on account of his strong grip, which he still had from when he busted broncs on that ranch over at Belle Fourche.

Howard called Webster every name in the book, but Webster felt that wind when Howard opened the door, and that's all it took. He'd been watching the snow in his headlights and remembering things he heard on the radio and TV about people being trapped in drifts and thirty thousand cows being frozen stiff and dead deer and pheasants all over the cornfields, and he wasn't going to let Howard go walking off. He knew Howard wouldn't walk a hundred yards before the wind turned him into a statue.

Howard wouldn't speak to him for about an hour after that, so he just talked to Dan. Sometimes he just let his mind whirl down into those other places spinning around in his head, spinning like the roulette wheel at Fort Randall Casino. Then he'd see the tips of eagle feathers turning in the sun in a slow circle. Then faster and faster, staggering back from the sacred tree, talons anchored in the flesh of his chest, pulling, tearing his flesh with the sun beating him senseless. The drum kept pounding in the center of his heart, he couldn't hear what Dan was saying, only the pounding in his ears, mustangs flashing on the planes of a dream Webster was painting on a piece of buffalo skull. A hot wind blew across his face, the odor of blood-scented grass. When the talons tore loose, he fell into snow deep as wounds in the bodies of women and children lying dead in the ice at Wounded Knee. When he touched them, they changed into otters, speared and wriggling in the snow.

Webster said it was like feeding sticks to a fire keeping his mind alive, fighting to stay awake after Dan quit talking, too, and the silence pressed harder on his skull. He curled around the fire in his brain while the Falcon rocked and bucked in the wind. He fed more sticks, thinking of sticks he and his two sisters, Katrina and Lois, fed to the fire in their cabin near DeSmet when he was nine. That was the winter of 1949 when they used every scrap of wood and paper and old clothes and wooden toys and magazines and some encyclopedias the priest at DeSmet gave them. Then they had to start pulling pieces of wood out of the walls and floor to keep a little warmth and hold the chill outside the walls.

Webster could see the two gold carp his mother bought him at the Woolworths store in Platte, how the water in their bowl grew cooler and cooler, then iced over on the surface. Little spikes of ice crept down into the bowl until those fish were trapped in a block of ice, which Webster could hold up to the light or near the fire and make it flicker like a jewel.

Webster and his sisters played a game they called Jewel of the Nile from something Katrina read at school. One of them would hide the frozen fish, and the others would try to find them in the corners and cubbyholes of that four-room cabin. Losing themselves in the search and pretending they were in the jungles of South America. Jaguars were lurking behind every bush. That way, they could almost forget the cold, not pay attention to their mother and grandfather ripping insulation and slats of wood from the walls and feeding them to the fire while the old man muttered in Lakota about a deer he killed one time with a rock.

They practically peeled the place bare by the time that storm ended. Webster, he still remembers how he kept staring at an icicle the sun was melting when the storm stopped, and then he saw a magpie flash across the yard and land on a tractor seat poking out of the snow.

Old Webster, he had the mind for it, you know, for being stuck in a blizzard in the dark on the coldest night of the year. He had the mind for it, and the eyes, too, and when he wasn't trying to get Dan or Howard to keep talking or telling them jokes and when he wasn't walking the trails of his dreams, he was watching the things the wind was doing to drifts or watching the way ice was bubbling to a dull blue glaze on the windshield. He kept scrunching down, trying to tell if he could feel any movement in his toes. His feet were numb, out away from his body, somewhere under the hood of the car. His feet were walking toward the little space heater Willard One Dog keeps in his barbershop.

Then Webster was pretending he could put his feet in the whirlpool they had in that gymnasium over to Woonsocket when he was in high school and how he would sit on the edge and soak his bad ankle after a football game. The ankle, it still hurt and was paining him, but he took the handoff from Dexter McCray and cut toward the hole off guard. He saw it was plugged and cut to the outside, peeling off Leo Little Bird's block and turning the corner. That field opened wide as the sky, and Webster sprinted down the sideline for the only touchdown they got against Sisseton. Sisseton beat hell out of them, 49–6, and two days later a storm blew in and locked down on the reservation, and Webster, he ran that touchdown in his head about forty times while he was shoveling snow or shivering in his bed at night

But like Webster says, you can only keep them wheels in your head running for so long and pretty soon they start slowing down and all the pictures get grainy, almost like your eyes are filming up, like so many of the elders' eyes gone cloudy as pipe smoke. So then he starts praying all them prayers the Jesuits taught him at the boarding school because he had that other side to him, you know, the stuff he got from the priests and nuns. Webster, he wasn't one to turn away from something that spoke to his spirit. It all fit together for him—the Lakota ways and the Christian ways—and he'd gotten a lot of peace from his Christian prayers when his daughter died from some sickness she picked up over in Desert Storm. That hurt him real bad because the army never could explain what happened to her and the people at the veterans hospital couldn't either, and so Webster had to just watch her die, there was nothing he could do.

He kept praying for her until morning came, and that's when he'd seen the man in the red sweatshirt sitting behind the wheel of the car. Webster figured it was his guardian angel sent to get him and Dan and Howard out of there. He tried to talk to the angel, but the angel wouldn't turn around. The sheriff's deputy that rescued Webster a little while later said there wasn't anybody in the front seat. Then it came out in the paper that Webster was probably hallucinating. When he read that in the paper, he just laughed.

Just before the deputy opened the door, Webster was starting to let go. He couldn't remember his name or the names of the two men on either side of him. He didn't know they were both dead, just thought they were too cold to move. He said it was so strange quiet in the car, and his brain was all grainy like a television set in a lightning storm, just a flicker of whiteness; then he realized the deputy was pulling him out of the car. For just a few seconds he felt warm again, and his eyes came back into his head, and he was damn glad to be back in real snow.

That's what makes the chicken leg Webster is holding up now, like some priest about to bless us with holy water, look so good to him. Just being back here with all of us and smelling the deep-fat fryer and the beer and the cigarette smoke and the women's perfume and the manure on people's boots is the best feeling Webster's ever had. It's got his head spinning he's so damn happy to be out of that storm, and we all clap and cheer and whistle and lift our beers in a toast to Webster World Turner when he sinks his teeth into that steaming chicken leg.

Stingray

CANDACE MCCLOUD JUST WANTS TO cruise out of Rapid City, South Dakota, on I-90 East at 7 a.m., munching the doughnuts and sipping the coffee she and her sister, Kelsey, have just purchased at a convenience store at the east edge of Rapid. She just wants to tell Kelsey about the amazing article she had found two nights ago under some cook books on her computer hutch—an article she saved from clear back to last November about a nineteen-year-old California surfer girl escaping the jaws of a great white shark off the shores of northern California. But before she can begin to tell the shark story, Kelsey starts scolding her about the Corvette Stingray they are riding in—a silver torpedo Candace purchased six weeks before this short road trip to the Badlands. So Candace just keeps still, munches her doughnut, sips her cappuccino while Kelsey tells her that she had no business buying a car like this; you can't afford it. Repairs will cost an arm and a leg; insurance premiums will be brutal. Worst of all, the engine will be so powerful it will tempt you to drive even faster than usual, and you'll end up wrapped around a telephone pole.

As soon as Kelsey ends her litany of warnings and reservations to take a breath, Candace punches the accelerator, throws both of them back in their seats, and begins a rapid fire rebuttal about not being some damn kid at thirty-one years old, about getting outside the box once in awhile, and about what this car can do, how utterly amazing it is. She feels a steady, controlled edge to her voice, raising her volume along with her candor as she lists the car's virtues like she's been selling Corvettes for years. Telling Kelsey how, on the 2003 C5Z06, which mimicked the 1963 Stingray's body style, Chevrolet got rid of the old, double-overhead cam engine and replaced it with a much lighter 385 horse LSI engine. Combined with upgraded brakes, a rigid fixed roof, a titanium exhaust system, and a carbon fiber hood, the stunning result is unprecedented handling. Then she raves about the designer transmission she recently programmed for maximum acceleration, and concludes by saying she's dreamed about having a set of wheels like this her whole life.

"You talk about this thing like it was a person," Kelsey says.

"The salesman told me Corvette owners bond with their machines. And he was right. Something comes over me behind this wheel."

"Slow down, will you?"

"We're on vacation. Lighten up!"

"You're freaking me out," Kelsey says. "There are a lot of things I want to do before I die."

"Such as what?"

"Such as Crazy Days at the Rushmore Mall next week."

"Nothing ventured, nothing gained," Candace tosses out flippantly. "Which reminds me, I have to tell you this story I read on MSN about a surfer and a shark out in California. It happened last fall."

"Why are you telling me about it now?"

"I thought I'd lost the article after I printed it out, but I found it the other night by accident."

"Shark stories creep me out."

"This one is worth hearing, believe me."

"Fine. Just don't get into the blood and gore too heavy."

"I won't. I promise."

She downshifts and sets the cruise control at eighty-five.

"Anyway, this nineteen-year-old girl and her surfer buddies decide to do some surfing at a place called Bodega Bay on the north central coast of California. A beautiful Wednesday morning in mid-October. So they head out—about ten of them—into this spot called Salmon Bay and this girl, Mia, decides to go a little farther out than the others."

"There always has to be one," Kelsey says.

"Don't knock it," Candace says. "She had the experience of a lifetime and lived to tell about it."

"I'm not sure I want to hear this."

"You do, I know you do. This is mind-boggling."

"Just get on with the story."

"OK, OK. She's paddling along on her board out there dead center in the middle of her life, not a care in the world, as she catches and rides a couple of waves. But something doesn't feel right. She's in only about ten feet of clear water, but it feels 'sharky.' Then the water starts to shift in a funny way, and that's when a great white shark hits her board from behind, takes a huge bite out of the board and out of her leg, and then starts circling the board."

"Oh, my God!"

"Yeah, she said it was straight out of *Jaws*."

"Don't tell me any more."

"Chill out, will you? This is the good part. The magic part. It takes her only a few seconds to realize that the attack is on, and she hasn't a snowball's chance in hell of getting away, especially with the other surfers twenty to thirty yards closer to the shore. She can see the shark moving around her in a horseshoe, and all of a sudden her adrenaline kicks in, and she jumps on its back between the dorsal fin and the tail fin. She starts pushing on its back with her hands, like she's trying to shove it into the ocean, except she said later she was just trying to keep its mouth away from her body."

"If you're messing with me on this . . ."

"Not in the least. All her surfer buddies are paddling like crazy out to help her when they see the fin above the water. Then they see the shark kind of thrashing around just before it rolls over on its side, flashing its white belly, and first thing you know, it dives away, with the leash from the girl's board in its mouth. It would have taken her out to sea except that the leash broke and she was able to get back on her board, and they towed her back to shore with her mangled leg hanging off the board."

"I don't like the ocean," Kelsey says. "You wouldn't catch me out there, especially in a place that's known for sharks."

"But it turned away. Left her floating there. How weird is that? Mystical even."

"She just got lucky. There's nothing mystical about it."

"I disagree. The guys who examined the bites on her calf and thigh estimated that shark at eighteen to nineteen feet and four thousand pounds. And she jumps on its back. How would that feel? Can you imagine? It was beyond all logic. A glimpse of eternity."

"Now I know how that guy sold you this car," Kelsey says, tilting her seat back and closing her eyes.

"That's all you have to say?"

"All for now."

"You're hopeless."

"No, I'm a hostess. Don't worry, Candace. The story was great. I'm sure I'll have nightmares to match."

Candace is feeling more light-hearted now, so she turns on the high-powered sound system and cranks the volume, eager to have the music peel away a few more layers of the daily grind tedium of her job as a photographer for the *Rapid City Journal*. She got a good start last night by drinking herself under the table at Diamond Lil's in Deadwood, but knew when she woke this morning it was going to take something more to clean her vents. So she had just stood in the shower, singing "It's gonna be a bright, bright sun-shiny day" until the hot water ran out.

And a bright, sun-shiny day it is. The sky is a cloudless blue vault, and the sun is pouring through the windshield. The landscape between Wasta and Wall is spotted with greenery, and the fields sweep away into the horizon in a geometric swirl of brown and gray streaks and squares. The Stingray is purring along like a rocket idling on a launch pad. She's tempted to press the gas pedal to the floor a couple times just to see how long it will take to crest one hundred miles an hour, but doesn't want to get Kelsey agitated any further; so she put her urges on ice for the time being.

● ● ●

Just outside Wasta, the weather changes quickly, the sky getting hazy in the sweltering heat and the air growing dim as the weathered fence posts.

"We're losing the sun," Candace says, liking the nihilistic ring of the sentence.

Kelsey grunts and pulls her cap down farther over her eyes. Candace reaches into her purse and takes out a package of licorice nibs. Tilting the box to her lips and dumping several in her mouth, she begins chewing them to shreds as she mulls the drudgery at her office, the stillborn photo assignments she's had lately. She is absolutely sick of shooting fundraising dinners and fiftieth wedding anniversary celebrations. And cheese-ball groundbreakings, with all the hardhats and gold shovels. Such posing and artifice. Photojournalists are supposed to record real life—people actually doing things, not pretending to do things. And worst of all is when you actually catch something happening naturally and then have copy desk editors crop—no, butcher—the photo and rewrite the caption. It's enough to make your blood boil.

By the time she takes the exit to the eighteen-mile scenic route through the Badlands, she is hearing severe windstorm warnings on the radio. This doesn't bother her much, but the odd, cider-colored tint of the sky and the black bellies of the clouds drifting up from Nebraska catch her eye.

She pays the park entrance fee and cruises down into the hallucinatory pink wrinkles of the Badlands, with all its tan and lavender ravines and its scorched sage and sand—a labyrinth of rock and scrub brush, a sunbaked haven for rattlesnakes and hawks. Every time she sees it, she feels as though something has fallen away from her, like she's left the twenty-first century and is time-traveling to another planet. She loves coming here. Nothing rubs the daily grind off faster. She pulls the car to a stop on an overlook and shuts the engine off. Kelsey sits up and yawns.

"The sun's back out," she says.

"They should've made *Starship Troopers* here," Candace says, her eyes devouring the scene, "instead of at Hell's Half Acre down in Wyoming. This is much more gnarly."

"I could see a bunch of alien insects liking it here," Kelsey says.

They study the rumpled, jagged mounds that wind in an endless maze into more dust-choked ravines and blistered rocks. Above it all, the sky to the east looks misty and gray, like rain clouds are drifting in. To the south, the horizon has buckled into grayish-green bands of clouds with ashen edges. Not the usual static clouds one sees drifting across the prairie; these have dipped toward the ground like a massive false ceiling and are rippling forward, as though attached to a mechanical roller. When she starts the car and backs out on the sightseeing road, she says something about how the clouds remind her of a river, the even way they're flowing.

"Sort of sharky," she says, winking at her reflection in the driver's side window.

"You're such a drama queen," Kelsey says after eyeing the same stretch of sky. "Let's just get out of here. Get into a motel at Kadoka. There's been a lot of tornadoes this spring over in East River, and down in Nebraska."

"I've never seen a real tornado," Candace says casually. "I'd love to shoot one."

When she reaches the freeway entrance, the sky to the south is boiling like a cauldron and turning the most intriguing shades of green and black she's ever seen. She swings out on the freeway and prods the gas pedal. The car hugs the road with a fierce grip, and it feels like they are boring to the center of the earth on a gleaming steel track.

Seconds later, Kelsey sees a funnel cloud forming on a distant flat east of the car.

"Step on it," she yells. "It's a fricken twister!"

To Kelsey's shock and horror, Candace cuts her speed at the next exit, veers onto a state highway, then turns the Stingray in the direction of the funnel cloud.

"You're going the wrong way!" Kelsey yells.

"Don't wimp out on me now," she yells back. "Get my camera off the shelf behind you . . ."

"Do what?"

"My camera. Get my bloody camera out of the leather case on the shelf behind my seat."

"You're going to get us killed."

But Candace is not listening. The Corvette is rock steady at one hundred miles per hour. They could be sitting on a couch in her apartment, drinking a margarita. She forgets the margarita, though, when she whips around a long curve and sees the stringy black tail dangling from the clouds drop down to take on the conical shape of all holy terror and darkness. It swells quickly into a gargantuan top some malevolent deity has spun, and as it widens and grows, it turns a blood-chilling shade of gray.

She knows she shouldn't stop on the shoulder of the road, but the road goes up an incline at that point, and she suddenly sees a shot she can't resist.

"What are you doing?" Kelsey cries. "Turn the car around, for God's sake!"

Her words bounce off Candace, fade away somewhere in the bellow of wind outside the car. Kelsey doesn't exist; can't be allowed to exist. The world has stopped, and the tornado is simply spinning furiously in one spot. So she leaves the engine running, jumps out of the car, runs over to a fence rail where she can brace her elbows on the lumpy wood, and clicks off as many shots as she can before the funnel cloud wobbles slightly and begins to creep forward. She scrambles back to the car, jumps in, and throws the transmission in reverse

"Hang on," she shouts. "I'm doing a U-y."

Kelsey's mouth opens but no sound comes out. Candace wrenches the steering wheel to the left and guns the engine. In the rearview mirror, Candace can see the tornado gaining, flinging shed roofs, fence posts, and dirt in the air as it picks up speed.

She's known people who talked to their cars, patted the fenders as though the cars were some kind of old cow pony, but has never quite understood such a mindset until now when she finds herself whispering desperately to the Stingray, "C'mon, Sweet Baby Ray, cook it."

It is a narrow, two-lane road, but new asphalt has been recently poured; she decides to floorboard the gas pedal. The shadow of the tornado is darkening the road close behind when the Stingray's jets kick in and the car suddenly separates from the shadow, and then shoots like a bullet into the horizon. When Candace next looks in the rearview mirror, the tornado is gone. Then she spots it careening toward some bluffs to the west, and lets off the gas.

"We're alive, Sis, alive! And I can't wait to get back to Rapid and process those photographs. I caught that monster frozen in its tracks."

"How much pot have you been smoking lately?"

"Out of sight shots," Candace says.

"And what do you think you're going to do with them?"

"Don't know. But one thing is for sure. You're not going to see them in the *Rapid City Journal*."

She eases off the gas, switches the radio off.

"I'm sorry I put you through that, Kelsey. I couldn't help myself."

"Don't worry about it. I actually enjoyed the screaming. I can't do that at Applebee's, you know."

They look at each other in the tranquil, sunlit safety of the car and start to laugh. The more they laugh, the more relief they feel, and soon they are settled back into the mundane motion of the day. About five miles down the road, they stop laughing and chattering and lapse into a brooding silence for the next sixty miles. Then they stop for a buffalo burger and a beer at Al's Oasis in Chamberlain before heading back.

Candace engages the rocket burst rhythms of the Stingray's engine on some of the straight stretches, shifting and steering with the same abandon she indulged in going east. The one difference is that whenever Kelsey dozes off, she eases off on the gas and takes quick, eagle-eyed glances in the rearview mirror as though something is gaining on her in a fierce, rapid swallowing of distance. After the second or third glance a voice from deep within her, so deep she almost doesn't recognize it, is saying to her in an echo chamber mantra: "Eternity sucks, eternity sucks . . ."

She stops glancing in the rearview and focuses on the road ahead and the play of light above it. The sky is a pulsing blue arch, and the fields, ravines, and sun-scorched hillsides look pristine and undisturbed. In fact, they look fabulous.

Bottom Dweller

A CATFISH MUCH OLDER AND larger than the catfish Jessica Briggs has just dragged into a boat on a river in South Dakota hunkers in the warm, murky current of a reservoir dam near Elk City, Kansas. The Kansas cat's whiskers twitch like antennae above the olive silt, fish line trailing from hooks embedded in its jaw and lips as its thick, tubular body meanders below the fleeting world. Its ancient eyes filter the mud-colored movement of its feeding ground, and its fins flit and tremble, sending cryptic signals five hundred miles north to an old man dying in a Meckling, South Dakota, nursing home.

● ● ●

Chester Briggs, deep in a coma brought on by a blocked carotid artery, sees in his mind's eye another catfish, his own trophy cat, cruising muddy channels in the James River, its glossy gray back and wide, flat head oblivious to the world above as its whiskers sniff the bottom for food. Up and down the river this channel cat, or some facsimile of it, has drifted for thirty years or three thousand years, old as the striated sea bed's layers of rock and clay, sliding under beaver dams, its flanks and fins and whiskered face getting larger and larger while the world above rages on.

Above the river-bottom grazing grounds of Chester's channel cat the world has been burned black with bombs and smoke, buildings spewing fire, soldiers falling and vanishing in the forests and fields of Europe, bodies strewn on beaches, tide rushing out. The catfish dreams of fire and crumbling walls, waves its maestro whiskers with brute resolve, orchestrates the dropping of a bomb. The catfish is an enzyme in the world's befouled belly, helping earth digest the bones of men. It hovers in the timeless pull of gravity and stone, dines on detritus its barbels scent, its long, languorous body sniffing through the taste buds in its skin.

Chester's cat is a silver-skinned appetite, a mouth, a hungry god. It swims to eat and eats to swim and balks at the whiff of stinky cheese hooks rained down from the sky, then turns and swerves below a log or algae-covered ledge. The seasons come and go, and the river channels shift from blue to black to amber tints of waterlogged leaves tumbling through the current like disembodied fins, drifting past its feckless eyes. Beneath the shield of its back and the plate of its massive head it sorts dead shapes and smells, hangs comatose in log-darkened pools.

The fish that Chester Briggs is dreaming about weighed fifty-eight pounds when he caught it in 1959 with a wooden pole and minnow bait. Chester is feeling the hook set now, the catfish tugging slowly at first, then pulling with the power of a hardcore eddy. All around Chester the humid South Dakota summer balloons with heat and insects, the brackish odor of backwater, red-winged blackbirds strafing through cattails and reeds. Chester sees, feels the rush of the world above—the bright, burning distance, the violet ridges of bluffs, the jungle of corn. When he yells, "It's a big one!" his voice arrows over the road, gets swallowed by the sweltering ears of corn.

But he doesn't care who hears him. His mind has dived under the water now, and he is seeing the catfish of catfish, the one he's waited almost twenty years to catch. He had to stop fishing while he was in the army, fighting the Japanese in the Philippines, hacking his way through the jungle, firing his rifle in mad wild bursts at the wavering wall of trees. And all around him, the burning huts, the naked children running, the tropical birds on fire, feathers torn from their blackened bodies drifting in the shadows of palms. A three-year-hiatus of bullets and blood before he came back to the catfish, back to fishing for channel cats and blues, the kind of meal a man of his station in life would only describe as "the best damn eatin' there is"—a catfish breaded and fried in the wild.

The blocked artery and the emphysema that have sacked Chester's lungs and weakened his heart drove him from the riverbank, forced him indoors, left him sweating and delirious in the small stucco house he lived in on the outskirts of Yankton. All his family dead or in rest homes or off to Arizona or California, except for Jessica, the one niece who lived up near Mitchell.

Jessica had refused to leave South Dakota, to leave the fishing and pheasant hunting. She would come down to see him whenever she could get time off from her job teaching mathematics at Dakota Wesleyan in Mitchell, her not minding the sparsely furnished house or the sour scent of blood caked on the boots and pants Chester wore to his job at Cimple Meats. Or she'd loop down during paddlefish season at Lewis and Clark Lake and stop in to tell him what she'd caught. She was the only relative he had left in the state—his favorite niece whom he'd taught everything he knew about fishing. Not just catfish but perch and walleye and even those vicious Northern Pike. But it was catfish that fired her imagination, made her taste buds go crazy. He'd taught her how to cook them, too, how to deep fry them in cornmeal and rice flour, how to eat them like you had forever to do it.

He could almost taste the flesh of channel cats in his wobbly, intermittent dreams, could smell the scent of them frying beside a moon-flashing stream. Now and then the record-setting cat he'd caught in 1959 swam into view out of distant shadows, its boulder-shaped head and bottom dweller's body cruising toward him, swimming into the flash of Lucas Hawk's camera. The shot had been taken outside Hawk's bait shop, the state record photograph now under glass at the Missouri River Aquarium, the photo part of the same display as the mounted fish.

There had never been a grander photo than that photo, nothing from the family album that could touch it. The mounted catfish itself he was not as pleased with or proud of. The taxidermist had altered some of the fish's coloring in an attempt to glamorize the fish in that glassed-in coffin flooded with fluorescent light, but had ended up making the fish less real, less grand in all its earthy ugliness. There was really nothing glamorous about a catfish, though he had not forgotten the magic of its body the day he pulled it from the James River and stood there staring at it in the hazy white light of the prairie.

Twisting to find a comfortable position in his bed at Prairie View Convalescent Center, Chester sees the big cat coming out of the water, bursting like some fat gray god into a world of light and air, streaks of water blazing on its back and tail. It hangs there on the treble hook, him seeing it all at once and in miraculous detail: the bloodspot in its eye, the red rosette below its gill, the saber swerve of its whiskers, the shimmering rays of its tail . . .

● ● ●

. . . while Jessica, stunned by the size of the catfish she has just pulled out of the James River only a few miles from the nursing home, can't be sure it's a record breaker, but knows it could be, it could be. She works to bring her catch into the boat, to watch its awkward death throes and listen to its thunderous flopping when it jerks out of the net and searches for water on the boat's wooden floor. She thinks momentarily that it will knock the sides out of the boat, snap the line, dive back into the river, and disappear.

But it doesn't escape, and half an hour later she is roaring down a gravel road in her pick-up, the catfish covered with ice in her largest cooler as she races toward Meckling. He won't believe this, she thinks, oh my God, he'll be so happy to see this. Her uncle Chet has never talked much, especially during the past six months as his condition has worsened, but the few times he's talked with her at any length it's been about fishing, about where to find the best catfish, what bait to use, how she has to be patient: "You gotta think like them, like you got all the time in the world."

Jessica knows she doesn't have all the time in the world. The old man's coloring has deteriorated to an amber gray, sometimes almost green, the tints of his face reminding her of fish she's drawn up to the edge of a boat, his mouth but a fleshy hole and the bruised-looking skin below his ears twitching like gills. But this fish will bring back his color, will give him the face she has always loved, the eyes she trusts more than any other eyes. The fish will be better than any flowers or gift she could buy from a store, any medicine the nursing home staff could offer him. It will finish things out in the right spirit—1959–1989—as one moment with no years in between. Almost too good to be true.

Which is what she thinks the instant she sees him lying dead on his back in the nursing home bed. Two nurses stand in the hallway behind her, having held their tongues and tempers when she entered the lobby with a massive fish in her arms, its great forked tail making both of them think of a whale's flukes. Water spots on her shirt, the thighs of her jeans soaked, water dripping on the hardwood floor as she barged past their slow reflex attempts to stop her. And the nurses creeping in cautious silence down the hall to watch as she entered the room and approached the bed.

In death he is surprisingly reposed. The color has returned to his cheeks, and his features are relaxed, though slightly waxy in the evening light. His hands are at his sides, and his thin, sinuous body lies perfectly flat beneath the sweat-soiled sheets.

Jessica starts to tell him about the catfish she is holding more tightly than anything she's ever held, to say something like, "You won't believe what I did today." But she can't find the voice to say anything out loud. Then it occurs to her that he would believe what she did today, that he was expecting her to catch this fish, that he can see it plain as day, water from its porous skin mixing with her tears and pooling on the squares of linoleum between her feet.

After making arrangements with the nursing home administrator on where to take her uncle's body, Jessica walks out to her pick-up, places the catfish back in the cooler, and fastens the lid. She knows she should get the fish home soon and clean it. She knows that she will be having a fish fry on Friday night for a few of her uncle's friends who can still get around. They will feast the night away, down to the cartilage and bones.

* * *

The catfish lying at the base of a dam in the middle of Kansas knows nothing of this story or the people in it. They are but vibrations from above the swirling surface of the tailwaters it dwells in, registered with blind patience in the quiver of its barbels. That world is but a slice of light in which tiny figures move much like the transient pieces of dead matter this catfish has devoured in reaching 105 pounds. Across a large portion of the twentieth century, the commotion of the world above has drifted over the silt-laden sanctuary of this fork-tailed demigod, who, wiser than the most ingeniously baited hook, the most provocative smell, is drawn to other things, to dreams of other things. The events of the world above are like maverick flashes of light, little nightmarish twists of the inklings it expels with it feces. Of greater importance, of far greater attraction is the never-ending lure of river bottom rocks.

part ii:
homesteader legacies

It was the last of autumn and the first day of winter coming together. All day long the ploughmen on their prairie farms had moved to and fro in their wide level fields through the falling snow, which melted as it fell, wetting them to the skin—all day, notwithstanding the frequent squalls of snow, the dripping, desolate clouds, and the muck of the farrows, black and tenacious as tar. Yet the ploughman behind his plough, though the snow lay on his ragged great-coat, and the cold clinging mud rose on his heavy boots, fettering him like gyves, whistled in the very beard of the gale.

—Hamlin Garland, "Under the Lion's Paw" in *Main Traveled Roads*

Whatever you do in life you are going to find people all around you faking and getting away with it.

If you have time some day, read again the last section of my "Story Teller's Story"—about the man who wrote football stories.

Fake men being acclaimed everywhere, fake furniture in houses, fake house building, city building.

Vast sums being acquired by men from fakiness.

That doesn't matter.

You can't fake raising corn in a field. Life comes back to the substance in the sod.

—Sherwood Anderson, from a letter to his son, John, 1927

Curse of the Corn Borer

DEWEY BRUNICK HAD BEEN SITTING for over an hour on the split leather stool at the end of the bar in the smokey Happy Hour light of Cleo's Lounge, thinking about worms. About what he knew about corn borer worms. Certainly more than anyone else in the place. More than any of the University of South Dakota students and professors who came and went in waves across the week-day Happy Hours, sucking down as many beers and gin and tonics as they could before the price went up at 6 p.m.

This evening was no different. The place was jammed with the returning college crowd and an occasional downtown office worker or farmhand, and the clink and clatter of glasses and taco bar dishes meshed with the crescendo of voices that swirled around Dewey and drifted into the hammered tin tiles on the ceiling as he ran the corn borer reels over and over in his mind.

It didn't bother him to sit alone at the end of the bar, obscure in his overalls and corn-seed cap, his eyes permanently bloodshot and a three-day growth of beard making him look like a weather-worn goat. It didn't bother him to see the sensual curves of the college girls, with their flirty voices and the heart-stopping beauty of their eyes and mouths. He looked at them across a canyon and paid only slight attention to the virile young men they were leaning into and rubbing up against, granting the young men their time, their turf. And knowing, at sixty-six, that the young women moved and laughed and swung their hips like figures in a dreamlike arcade. They were ten feet, twenty feet, sometimes two feet from him, but they were out of reach, walking naked on some other planet. Reaching across that distance, acting on his urges, was, he knew, futile.

So looking but not touching tormented him occasionally but not often. Far more bothersome were the conversations he'd been privy to for the past five years, ever since he'd quit drinking at Toby's in Meckling and switched to Cleo's Lounge. Like the bodies of women, most of the conversations glanced off him, vanished in the glare of sun on windshields when he pushed the front door open and staggered out to the 1985 Dodge pickup he parked at the end of the block. He would enter the waning glow of dusk, like a fish drifting into the green and yellow sway of an inland sea, climb into the cab of his pickup, roll the windows down, then flop over on the seat and snore until dark. He had the timing down perfectly—two hours and forty minutes to sleep off the bourbon he'd consumed during Happy Hour at Cleo's, then he'd be steady enough to drive out to the farm without getting pulled over.

But every now and then, a conversation would get under his skin—usually some professor showing off his knowledge of history or politics or economics. They had all the fancy words and names, all the complicated details, and it bugged him, made him feel like some beetle lurking in the shadows at the end of the bar. He had no desire to enter such conversations, feeling that there was nothing he could contribute, and he was damned if he would sit there and ask awestruck questions the way some of the students did. He had no clue what the professors were talking about most of the time, sometimes feeling dwarfed by the way they carried on, sometimes embarrassed that he'd gone only as far as the eighth grade before quitting school to work on his father's farm.

So Dewey had no education, at least not in the eyes of these people. But he knew things. He knew plenty of things. What he knew about was corn; tons of things—enough to fill several books. He knew even more about pests, about the incredible war between corn growers and worms. He'd been fighting that war for forty years. He hadn't gone off to Europe like his two older brothers, who were both buried somewhere in northern France. The army wouldn't take him because of his flat feet, or he'd probably be poking up daisies in France himself. No, he stayed with the old man; he became a corn grower, as good a corn grower as any man in Union County, maybe the best corn grower in Union County.

It was because he'd gone to school in worms. He had no diplomas, degrees, or titles, but he had knowledge. He had paid for it with sweat and backache and worry and with trial and error. With his life. Some nights, lying in the heat-bloated bedroom in the second story of his farmhouse and listening to the faint but agonizingly beautiful squeak of corn husks swelling in the tropical heat of August, he was overwhelmed with his understanding of corn and corn's great enemy, the corn borer worm.

Dewey was both proud and humble about what he knew about worms. And he was filled with an almost inexpressible regard for the cunning and adaptability of worms. Cut worms, wire worms, root worms, and the granddaddy of them all, the European Corn Borer. Now there was a worm. The smartest little devils he'd ever done battle with. In their own way they were geniuses, masters of survival. Sly as Houdini. Ruthless as Hitler.

He'd seen countless examples of their creative prowess, their determination to eat his corn. They put hailstorms and raccoons to shame. They were stunning, brutally simplistic in their concentration, in their reproductive frenzy. They had more moves than the wind. One example was the way the eggs could wrap up in a cocoon, convert cellulose to protein, and then saturate themselves in alcohol to ward off the bitter cold of Dakota winters. Come spring, they would climb out of those ravaged cornstalks and turn into moths, jamming the summer skies with their cinnamon-streaked wings and splattering their bodies on the windshields of cars and farm trucks until the glass was covered with wing dust and the sickening yellow gel of their eggs.

It was an amazing cycle to witness, to war against. It had taught him things he yearned to tell someone, but he rarely got a chance to share his knowledge. The occasional instances in which he managed to capture a Cleo's Lounge patron's attention, he'd see the light of interest waning in their eyes, catch them glancing elsewhere in the bar just before they jumped up and hollered someone's name, jarring him out of his focus and scrambling his nerves to where he had to down a double shot of Jim Beam before he could gather his wits and settle back into his singularity and isolation. At those moments, Dewey felt an odd kinship with corn borer larvae curled in an alcohol-induced stupor while the outside world raged on. Other times he'd hold their attention long enough to command a little respect—something in their looks or voices told him he had surprised them—this tattered old fart with his Camel cigarettes and his row of empty shot glasses. He could hold them to him long enough to make himself feel like he was actually sitting there, had done and seen things that mattered. But if the conversation slipped off track, veered into current affairs or pop culture, he faltered, fell silent, raised his intake of whiskey. Usually the talk turned to sporting events, which he had no interest in, having been forbidden by his father to participate in any organized sports in elementary school and having come to agree with his father over the years that sports were a waste of time. Or the conversation jumped to music or movies, and he was instantly at sea; the last film he'd seen being *Jaws* in 1976. Dewey remembered it well, considered it the best movie he'd ever seen, especially the part where that sheriff had yelled, "Die, you son of a bitch!" and then shot a bullet into a propane tank lodged in the shark's rear teeth, blowing him to kingdom come.

But no one ever wanted to talk about *Jaws*. A lot of the kids going to college now would smirk and look at each other, then ask him if he'd seen *Pulp* Something—some damn city thing about drugs and guns. Those were the times he found himself agreeing with the Russian professor who'd gotten smashed drinking shots of Prairie Fire one Thursday night last spring. Just before falling off his stool and hitting his head on the corner of a billiard table, the Russian professor had looked down the bar at Dewey and said, "They're not educable."

"Who?" Dewey said.

"American students," the professor said. "You can't teach them anything. They're like insects warding off pesticides, getting high on DDT."

Before Dewey had a chance to disagree, the Russian professor had looked deep into the bottom of his empty glass, set it disturbingly close to the edge of the bar, and then pitched off the stool, arms flat against his sides.

Thinking now about what the Russian professor had said as he looked over the crowded tables and lineup of young people seated around the U-shaped bar, Dewey still disagreed. The professor was wrong. These kids wanted to learn something. All kids want to learn something.

Why would anyone who didn't want to learn something go to college? It made no sense. The Russian professor was off base. It was just a matter of the kind of knowledge you offered them. Most of the stuff they were teaching now was hot air.

Social crap. Give them something real to sink their teeth into, and they'd eat it up. He had thought this through a number of times since the night the professor had fallen off the barstool, and he sensed that sooner or later he'd have to prove the professor wrong.

To Dewey's surprise and half-drunken delight, the opportunity presented itself ten minutes later when a tall, thin young woman in a tank top and cut off jeans spun to her left to face what Dewey guessed to be a Coyote football player, and yelled, "Fuck off, Kyle! I've had enough of your tight-ass behavior."

"Screw you, too, Justine," the hulking young man said, waving an empty beer bottle in her face. "I have half a mind to shove this up your ass."

"Don't flatter yourself," Justine said, "by thinking you have half a mind."

"Bite me, bitch," the football player said, slamming his bottle down on the bar. Then he plowed through the crowd like an angry water buffalo, knocking the door open with a forearm, and was gone.

For a moment she stood there with her hands on her hips, Dewey taking in her shapely legs. Then she let out a large sigh, climbed back on the stool, and pointing at her beer mug while eyeing the bartender, said, "Hit me, Chuck."

When the bartender brought a new mug of beer, Dewey slid his stool a little closer and tossed a five-dollar bill on the bar.

"On me," he said, catching the young woman's eye.

Her face, still chiseled into a hatchet from her lover's quarrel, softened suddenly, and a smile gradually transformed her features. Dewey wavered, felt the magnetic pull of her dark-brown eyes.

"How nice of you. Thank you."

"My pleasure," Dewey said. "Sounds like things aren't going so well for you."

"Oh, him," she said. "He thinks I'm sleeping with everyone in Vermillion. He has no right to . . . well, never mind. Let's talk about you instead."

"Me?"

"Sure. Why not? What's your name?"

"Dewey."

"Dewey what?"

"Brunick."

Her face suddenly lit up.

"I've heard of you," she said.

He straightened up on the stool.

"No dirt," she said. "The girls at the house talk about Cleo's a lot. They all seem to know you."

"I'm just a fixture here," he said. "Like a beer sign."

"Oh, c'mon," she said. "I've been wanting to meet you."

"What are you studying in school?" he said, confused by her attentive warmth.

"Pre-Med. Bio."

"Biology, eh?"

"It sucks. I've been thinking about switching to theatre. That was my other love in high school."

"What's wrong with biology?"

"Oh, I don't know. All the memorization. It's such a pain in the ass. School isn't even started yet, and I'm already bored."

She took another drink of beer, adjusted the straps on her halter top.

Dewey kept his eyes on her face.

"Are you a farmer?" she said suddenly.

"Do I look like one?"

"Yes, you do. Hey, why the long face? I like farmers."

"Really?"

"Hell, yes. They feed the world, don't they?"

"I never thought of it that way."

"What kind of farming do you do?"

"Corn mostly. And soybeans."

She nodded, took another sip of beer.

"I don't feel like going back to the house," she said. "Tell me something about growing corn."

"You're joking."

"No, I'm not. I'm all ears. Get it?"

He was holding a glass of bourbon in his cupped hands, tracing its rim with a greased-stained thumb.

"I don't know where to start."

"It doesn't matter," she said. "Start anywhere. Tell me what you know."

For the next hour, Dewey told her what he knew about corn. It was a little scattered at first, but then it all fell together, and he sailed forward, his whole being teeming with information. His mind split open like a cornucopia of hybrid corn and corn borer moths and dusty roads and algae-covered ditches, and he laid out the story of his life, minus all the social and personal facts. He configured the story instead in observations on the environment, the balance in nature, the hit-and-miss struggle to control the European corn borer in its assault on his crops, his livelihood. He explained everything he could think of, talked about cutworms, root worms, wire worms. Told her about the refuge corn patch the US Government made him grow, made all the farmers grow in sacrifice to natural balance. How 20 percent of his crop was raised without pesticides, without any genetically-altered seeds so that the corn borers would not become extinct.

Talked about how you have to be careful not to destroy a species because we don't know what part a species plays in the big scheme of things. He told her about the farmers in south-eastern South Dakota deciding to eradicate milkweed in the 1990s, how no one could see any purpose for that ugly, stinking plant. So they bombed it with Roundup, exterminated it with a vengeance. There was hardly any milkweed left now. But there were also no more migrations of Monarch butterflies, sweeping down the corridor of the Northern Plains and gracing towns large and small with their beautiful black and orange wings. Thousands of Monarch butterflies lighting up the landscape as they sought the syrupy nectar of milkweed heads. It was a classic example, a sad story, and Dewey told it well, wanting the young woman to understand, to appreciate the human mistake and its consequences in nature, its impact on all of us.

He had thought also to tell her about the days before BT corn, the crop-dusting chemical days when they fought the European corn borer with Puridan and other heavy metal derivatives, killing some of the corn borers but certainly not all. Killing in addition hundreds of swallows, the only natural enemy of the corn borer. But he sensed she was growing tired of hearing about corn, sensed they were both becoming too drunk to care. So he wrapped up by repeating how damn smart corn borer worms are, how you can't fool them with BT corn beyond five years and have to switch to a new, worm-resistant strain, how you can't even outfox them with rotational planting or with leaving a field dormant for a year because somehow by God they sense what you're doing, and they stay in the ground for another year, waiting until you plant more corn. Before there was so much corn growing, he told her, there were no corn borers. It was like the corn had created them, lured them out of the sky.

"This is getting pretty deep," she said. "It's time for me to go. But thanks for letting me in on all that stuff."

"The pleasure is mine," Dewey said.

She adjusted the waistline on her shorts, brushed the hair away from the sides of her face, then reached down and grabbed the braided-cloth bag hanging from a strap on her shoulder. She set the bag in her lap, opened it, and took out a vinyl coin purse. She squeezed the ends to make it open, reached in, and pinched something out of it with her thumb and forefinger. She dropped the coin purse back in the bag, let the bag slide back over her hip, and turned to Dewey.

"Open your mouth," she said.

"What for?"

"I want to give you something. My knowledge for your knowledge."

Dewey was an alcoholic, but he had always been wary of drugs. Tonight, though, he was so elated at having been listened to attentively that he grinned, shook his head, and stuck out his tongue. The young woman set a fat, furry tablet of some kind on it and quickly handed him her beer mug.

"Down the hatch," she said.

Dewey took the mug and washed the tablet down. The tablet was even larger than he had at first thought, and intensely bitter, and he had trouble swallowing it the first time; so he took two more big swallows of beer. He felt the tablet pass down his throat with the second swig, but then sucked a little beer into his lungs accidentally and broke into a fit of coughing that had him bent toward the floor for several minutes. When he looked up, the young woman was gone.

●　●　●

Dewey woke chilled on the seat of his pickup three hours later. He didn't know how long he'd lain there, couldn't see the numbers on his watch, which, in the dim interior of the cab were just blurred, iridescent splotches. From chilled he felt sudden-

ly warm as he gazed up at the neon sign above the tanning
salon he was parked in front of, its red and blue lines wavering like dancing snakes leaping toward the sky. He thought
for a few seconds he was going to vomit—something he never
did, no matter how much bourbon he drank—so he grabbed
the steering wheel and pulled himself to a sitting position. A
wave of dizziness twisted the parking meters and warped the
storefront windows on either side of the pick-up, then faded
away, and he felt suddenly lucid, taut in the brain. His senses
were keening to every crack and chip on the windshield, every streak of dirt and insect guts smeared in random patterns
across the glass.

Glancing to his right, he saw some college students staggering out the front door of Cleo's, their loud, drunken voices
muffled as though spoken from the far end of a swimming
pool. He glanced at his watch again, seeing this time that it
was only a few minutes past midnight. He could still get home,
sleep this bender off, and be out checking his corn for pests by
7 or 8 a.m. He knew he could get out to the farm safely, keep
the truck tracking the balding asphalt of the old back road he
took to avoid cops and other cars. He'd never had a DUI and
was not about to get one. He was awake and steady, though his
head hurt and his jaws ached as if he'd been clenching them
while passed out on the seat. But his hands and eyes were
sound, ready to perform.

Two or three miles out of town, Dewey turned off on what
he thought was his favorite back road, tunneling rapidly into
a corridor between walls of corn at peak growth, the stalks
dense and towering and glistening in the suffocating glow
of a summer moon. From the increasing waves of corn borer moths swarming over the road, he guessed this to be Ben
Heine's refuge corn patch—the 20 percent that Uncle Sam re-
quired all corn farmers to leave unprotected as kind of peace

offering to the European corn borer. Refuge patches were a consolation prize corn borers could devastate to their heart's content, insuring them their place in the ecosystem.

He could see the damage in the crippled stalks, ears drooping, the ground littered with ravaged ears, which seemed to be writhing in the dirt and sprouting wings with terrifying acceleration. The moths were rising in fluttering clusters and slamming into his windshield, which began to darken with their black bodies and streaks of yellow eggs. Strings of silver fire flaked off the moon, which hovered over the fields and road.

Closer and closer the moon came, with its flaming face pressing against the windshield, baking hundreds of moth bodies on the glass, fusing them in a crust Dewey couldn't remove with the wipers. He slowed down, tried to drive with his head out the window, but moths began to splat against his cheeks and forehead, clot his eyes with the pale dust of their wings, sprinkle eggs in his ears and nostrils.

When he drew his head back in, he glanced at the fields on his right where the cornstalks were turning into Lakota warriors wielding hatchets and spears, their auburn bodies painted with bright yellow dots and glowing blue bars. When they lifted their arms, their arms became wings, and they rose, arching into the night sky or dangling over the hood of the truck with scaly, bleeding feet, which he glimpsed through the remaining clear spots. Before long the spots were darkened with the phosphorescent gel of a million eggs, and he could see nothing.

Suddenly he left the road, feeling the front of the pick-up plunge into the ditch and the whole truck tilt down as he tried to brake. Weeds and rocks scratched and thumped against the undercarriage as he careened down the slope. In a desperate attempt to see where he was going, he turned the wipers to emergency speed, scraping enough dead moths off a narrow band of glass so he could see to crank the wheel enough to miss a large cottonwood stump. But then he dropped again down a slope that carried him out into an open field.

Dewey could see the barn coming, but in his confusion and free-falling emotions he pressed the gas pedal instead of the brake. He swerved at the last second, clipping the corner of the barn and shooting out into the field beyond the barn, coming to rest in a patch of soybeans when the engine died.

His mind was still flooded with dust devils spitting out corn silk and with the pink, wrinkled faces of bats, and he was gasping for air, his face dripping with sweat and the cab filled with the odor of fermenting corn. He knew he was on dry land but felt like he'd sunk to an ocean floor, kept expecting to see a school of brightly colored fish flit past the window. When he finally caught his breath, the whirling pictures in his mind faded to black, and the night went still as a stone, the air steaming with humidity and the moon sinking back into the distant void.

Dewey waited, staring at the rippled lava on the windshield and trying to place himself. The barn he'd clipped seemed familiar, but he couldn't be sure whose land he was on. It had to be one of his neighbors; he wasn't that far from home. Just as he was about to climb out of the truck to see if he could figure out where he was, the warm spot in his stomach surged with a writhing heat, and he knew he was going to vomit.

He elbowed the door open, half-stepped on the running board and fell awkwardly to the ground, scrambling to his hands and knees so he could brace himself for the vomiting. His fingers clawed the soybean plants and dug into the moist black dirt as he emptied out. When he hit the dry-heave point, he eased back on his haunches and looked out in front of him. That was when he saw the monster worm.

It lay in the dirt and weeds no more than twenty yards away; its massive body stretched out behind it forty or fifty feet and its mottled skin tinted an aquamarine blue in the moonlight. At first he could not believe such a worm could exist, and he tried to blink it away, but it remained—huge and ugly, the King Kong of Corn Borers. When he tilted his head, he thought he could hear its hideous mandibles mincing, crushing a hundred, a thousand ears of corn. Its eyes, in their flat black coldness, were older, nastier than the eyes of a great white shark.

Dewey felt a sudden wave of terror, an icy chill surging through his blood, felt his muscles tighten almost to paralysis. He knew then that he'd been born to kill this worm. Alone in that moon-blazing bean field, he was going to have to bring this bastard down. This thought seemed to melt away his fear, his hesitation, and he felt a sudden calm deep in the core of his being. Keeping his eyes on the giant corn borer worm, he crawled backwards slowly, reaching the pick-up and creeping up into the cab to lift his rifle off the rack mounted above the rear window.

He was glad he had kept it loaded because the worm would have less time to charge, less time to swallow him, and maybe the truck, before it ravaged the fields behind him, the beautiful prime crop acres of BT corn he'd planted to ward off corn borers. He knew that even BT corn could not resist this beast. It was a worm from Hell—the worst possible nightmare of mutation—and he understood now why he and the other corn growers had gone along with the 20 percent sacrifice plan. There was no telling what you might create by exterminating a species. Even then, something had gone wrong. The sacrifice plan hadn't worked.

His mind was starting to waver and jumble again, and he thought he heard the first rock band he'd seen at Cleo's singing, "*Stop, heyyyy . . . What's that sooounnnnd? Everybody look what's goin' rouuuund . . .*" The music faded, screeched off like a tape being eaten by a malfunctioning tape player, and Dewey was hearing the worm again, making a faint hissing sound. When he glanced out the windshield, the streaks of moth eggs re-formed into lava and wrapped their transparent wings around them as they wallowed in the cellulose they'd turned into capsules of alcohol. And then he saw himself in one of the cocoons, his bald head shining in the sealed booze.

He looked down at the rifle in his hands, reached deep inside himself, and turned to face the worm. He slid cautiously out of the cab, stood sideways in the shadow of the truck, and sighted on the worm's disgusting face. The worm's body seemed to tremble, its pale green and yellow markings barely distinguishable beneath the shimmering blue slime of its afterbirth.

When it raised its head, Dewey fired the first shot. Then a second, a third, square into the gray plate between the worm's eyes.

The worm absorbed the bullets and began to move forward. Dewey ran out in front of the pick-up, dropped to one knee, yelled, "Die, you son of a bitch!" and emptied the magazine into the worm. Before he could re-load, he felt a wave of dizziness and a tremendous weight dragging him to the ground. He dropped the rifle and passed out.

The chirping of birds and a glaring sun woke him. Lying there in the mud, he remembered almost nothing of the night before, only that he'd given that college girl at Cleo's the best lesson of her life. He could still see the look on her face. That was one lecture she wouldn't forget. He sat up and looked over at the barn near the road. Then he wondered what he was doing on Randy Mollet's land. He vaguely recalled turning one cottonwood tree too soon on Greenfield Road.

Standing up, he looked curiously at a long string of round hay bales only a few yards away. Randy Mollet had told him down at the Gerryowen Feed Store earlier in the summer that he was going to arrange his bales a new way this year—end to end—in long fat tubes, each bale wrapped in heavy blue plastic. Stepping a little closer to the long snake of bales, he could see that that was exactly what Randy had done. He had wondered at the time if Randy was doing the right thing, switching from the single bales he'd been scattering across his fields for years. He could see that the front end of the tube was already spilling hay out of its center. Well, it was Randy's business what he did with his hay.

● ● ●

Dewey was surprised to see his rifle and several shell casings on the ground in front of his pick-up, but figured he'd probably opened fire on some coyotes. So he gathered the shells, dropped them in his pocket, put the rifle back on its rack, closed the door, and started the engine. Looking out at the sweep of green fields that seemed to run forever into the bright blue Dakota sky, he was anxious as he could be to get home and see how his corn was doing.

The Recovering Dairy Farmer

THE FIRST STEP OCCURS IN mid-February when the third blizzard in three weeks sweeps in out of Canada, and Vernon Nygaard, out checking his dairy barns and feed lot, finds four Holstein cows frozen to death in a heap of fur, horns, ice, and snow. The sight of their bulging, ice-glazed eyes, their twisted limbs, their purple udders pulls the curtain back on a montage of scenes that have haunted him the past six months, starting with the ice storms in November. Which were followed by the relentless snowstorms of December, the temperature plunges in January, and the collapsed pole barn roof, he and his wife, Karen, startled into a run from the milk parlor as pieces of shingle and steel, ice and snow came crashing down, killing three cows and injuring six others.

In spite of that disaster, Vernon's spirits had been buoyed up by a gathering of neighbors in his yard to help him free the remaining cattle from the debris and clean up the wreckage, raising his hopes and lifting the eyes of his wife and his two children, Walter and Mary Lynn. The boost carried him into sucking up his courage and determination to keep on milking, to tend to the surviving cows out in the open. All this before the second and third blizzards and the discovery he makes this morning: the grotesque heap of iced-over carcasses that tells him he's hit bottom.

● ● ●

The second step is Vernon's decision that same morning to take Dave Mortenson's advice and "Get away from here. Take a vacation. Go to Florida. For your sake, and for Karen's and the kids."

That night lying in bed on the second floor of the cantering gray Victorian house, cooling down from a lovemaking session with Karen, he proposes the breakaway—the escape to Sea World—to Karen, who, after telling him they can't afford a trip right now, changes her mind, gets his drift when he says, "We can't afford not to. I'm losing my mind, and we could lose this marriage." Sitting up on the edge of the bed to stare out the window, she says, "Let's do it. We'll find the money, and we'll get my brother to tend the cows."

* * *

The third step occurs a week later when the Nygaards head off to the Sioux Falls airport on a sunny, subzero morning for a trip to Orlando, Florida. The journey, the change of scene, seeming almost like a visit to another planet, turns out to be a wise move, a life-saving move, a balm on the soreness of all their emotions and spirits, lifting the weight of a fierce South Dakota winter off their necks and shoulders, at least momentarily. Walking through the exhibits, watching the whales and dolphins perform at Sea World, bodies arching, diving, rolling, and surfacing in 80 degree temperatures, sun flaming on their fins and white bellies, Vernon feels winter flake away like the pieces of water-bubbled paint on the side of his house. Riding the rollercoaster, they crest the terrifying track, tensing in unison before the suicidal plunge down the narrow, rattling track, looping up and backwards as though untangling himself and his life from the barbed wire of a Northern Plains winter.

* * *

The fourth step is a feeling of freedom and hope, a readiness to start again, try again. Karen is feeling it, too. There is a sense of the whole family coming back to the old unity, the unspoken confidence which had become so frazzled from chipping and scraping the arctic glaze of those two November ice storms, which locked the entire farm in a frozen gloss. And from shoveling December snowstorms around the clock, ice stiff as stone beneath the drifts, snowflakes falling through waking hours, through darkness and dreams. And from getting stuck on the roads and getting frostbitten fingers trying to pry the barn door open and break loose the frozen mounds of feed. And from praying at dinner and in their beds until their brainwaves flattened to a single mantra: *Please make it stop snowing.*

● ● ●

Vernon takes the fifth step on the airplane ride home while the family dozes in the claustrophobic cabin with its body odors and scant supply of oxygen. He sees in his mind's eye the pole barn collapsing again, sees the cattle buckling, vanishing, can hear their bawling through the rubble. And even though the insurance has covered some of the losses, it seems like someone is trying to tell him something; something is hissing a message through the winter wind. This is when he remembers the offer a farmer from Baltic made him two years ago—giving him some of the milk from fifty-two cows in exchange for housing them. He doesn't know if the Baltic farmer's offer still stands, but he can feel himself pondering it more seriously than he ever thought he would.

● ● ●

The sixth step comes in March when Vernon starts finding dead pheasants in his pastures and corn fields, when he sees deer coiled in circles of bone three or four yards from haystacks. Then the flooding begins, rivers jumping their banks from Fargo to Sioux Falls, fields ruined, bridges out, roads washed away, the world covered with mud.

In his own barns and fields, he finds aborted calves and lambs, the stillborn, glassy fetuses, eyes staring with the distant opacity of winter-born wounds. He begins losing more calves, the future of his herd sliding into oblivion with crumbling river banks.

*   *   *

The seventh step surfaces toward the end of March, the temperature rising daily, the sun getting fuller, redder on the prairie horizon. Trees are budding, and red-winged blackbirds perch on posts and mile markers along Highway 115. Drifts are melting, corn stubble poking from acres of snow-soaked dirt. The flowering plum trees lining the driveway are budded out, except for one near the gate, its winter-killed skeleton outlined against the glows of dawn and dusk. Gray and white kittens chase one another around the base of a birdbath he bought Karen for Christmas, while their charcoal-colored father chews on a squirrel he caught napping in the barn.

But Vernon Nygaard isn't springing toward spring. Lying awake on his twelfth straight night of insomnia he is trying to find an exact reason, a breaking point for the onslaught of his numbness of heart, for the buzzards perched in the lightning-charred snags of his eyes. As far as he can remember, he has coped with winter as his father coped, and his grandfather before him, and his great-grandfather before him—farmers all—with South Dakota winters. This is why he has moved away from the thought of calling the farmer from Baltic, the thought to quit milking.

● ● ●

The eighth step arrives with the morning paper, much of which Vernon reads in the poorly lit breakfast nook with a farmer's detachment, distrust, and amusement until he happens across an article about depression containing a chart that lists and describes seven major symptoms. Laying the paper down and staring out the kitchen window at the black silhouette of the dead plum tree, he realizes he has scored seven out of seven. He doesn't like doctors or hospitals and has never believed in psychiatrists, but he can feel the agitation, the accuracy of the chart that describes him to the letter.

He understands then why he's felt low as a snake's belly and cold in the heart; why he refused to take Karen to the St. Patrick's Day dance at the church; why he didn't drive north to help Leonard Hatch when his pole barn collapsed; why he'd lost interest in sex; why he'd quit stopping at the Sunshine Café in Avon to chew the fat with friends; why he'd lost thirteen pounds. He knows now why he has been entertaining ridiculous fantasies of taking off, catching a bus to Minneapolis or Chicago, not telling anyone he's going, changing his name, disappearing; knows why he didn't flinch or feel a thing when he heard that Derrick Weeden had lost a foot to frostbite from getting caught out trying to feed cattle in that final February storm; why he had no response when the family's black Lab got trapped under ice on the James River and drowned, the rest of the family in tears and upset for days while he stared at the Channel 13 weather report.

● ● ●

Step nine follows that afternoon when Vernon calls the farmer from Baltic to see if the offer still stands. The offer stands. He tells the farmer he will think it over, talk to his wife, which he does.

"Are you absolutely sure about this?' she says.

"Absolutely."

"And we'll stay on the land? I can't see you living in town, ever."

"I don't plan on living in any town. I plan on being buried at the Bluestem Cemetery. We'll stay right here. Only the one thing will change."

"What'll you tell the children?'

"The truth," he says. "They'll get it. They've been living here their whole lives. It's not like they haven't seen my reasons."

She looks at him, through him, down the long, windblown corridor of their marriage.

"All right," she says. "I'm with you."

● ● ●

Step ten involves yet another conversation with Karen, but this time over beers and a large plate of deep-fried calves' testicles at the Detour Lounge in Waubay, where they've combined a short fishing trip with the annual Sanford County Testicle Festival. The conversation taking place this time, amidst the smoke-clouded racket and the ding of poker machines is not about Vernon; it is about their son, Walter. Vernon has been telling Karen about his decision to talk Walter out of being a farmer.

"But that's all he talks about," Karen says. "It's the only thing he cares about other than fishing and deer hunting. Why would you do that?"

"I owe it to him," Vernon says. "To spare him the pain and madness. He'll be starting high school next year. I don't want him going into high school thinking none of it matters because all he's got to do is wait for the four years to be over, then go farm."

"What makes you think he doesn't care about his studies? He gets all As and Bs."

"I don't care what he gets. I've seen him in the milking barn. I've seen the look on his face when he gets out in the sticks with a bow and arrow. I've heard him talk about machinery he thinks is cool, and it's not Ford Mustangs."

"Well, at least he aspires to something good."

"True enough, but why can't he be like so many of the other guys' sons? There isn't one of them wants to stay on the farm. They can't wait to race off to the city and be engineers and lawyers; doctors even. They see where everything is going."

"I doubt that they see much more than the chests and back ends of sixteen-year-old girls," Karen says. "And just because they're doing it doesn't mean everyone has to do it."

"I'm still going to tell him," Vernon says. "I won't be able to forgive myself if I don't, and he ends up hating his life."

"Relax," Karen says. "Go ahead and talk to him. I think you should."

"Really?"

"Why not? You're his father. That's what fathers do."

"OK then," Vernon says, popping a testicle in his mouth and grinding it up with his molars before washing it down with a long swig of beer. "Wanna dance?"

Holding her close on the crowded dance floor while the cowboy band does a slow fiddle and guitar number, he can feel her breasts pressing into his chest, can feel the solid fit of his hand on her lower back.

"I love this damn place," he whispers.

She doesn't answer, and he can't see her face, but he can sense her smiling into his shirt.

● ● ●

Step eleven takes place a few days later when Vernon takes Walter for a ride in the old Chevy truck under the guise of checking fences and looking for washed-out bridges. He prefaces his main plea to Walter by repeating his decision to get out of hands-on dairy farming but reminds Walter that he will be staying on the farm himself. The point is to do what he says, not what he does.

"I obviously can't leave a place that's been in our family for four generations. But you know what we've been through with trying to run a milking operation the past couple years."

Walter says nothing, head turned slightly toward the hood of the truck. But he seems to be listening while Vernon runs through the list of reasons he should think about becoming something other than a farmer. Vernon is pleased with his explanations, arguments, and pleas, feeling the power of his convictions in his chest muscles and voice. He concludes by saying he wishes he didn't have to say these things, but it is for Walter's own good.

They've come to a stop on a rise overlooking the James River. Walter waits until the silence makes it clear that his father is finished talking, then looks at him with affectionate yet undaunted eyes, as though Vernon had just arrived from Mars or had been speaking to him in Greek or Latin.

"I'll think it over, Dad," he says, then turns to gaze down at the river valley, his voice lifting with urgency and wonder when he points out a small group of antelope grazing in a band of setting sun on a distant hillside.

Vernon, leaning back in the seat, relaxes his grip on the steering wheel. He locates the antelope just before they vanish in shadow, and he realizes then that there is nothing he can do. The damn kid loves the land.

● ● ●

In taking step twelve, Vernon takes the biggest step of all. He accepts his son's decision.

Big House on the Prairie

Fitch

That damn Kyte. He was all for the trees at the beginning, thought it was a great way to make some extra money. Said them evergreens would grow into first class Christmas trees, and first thing you know, we'd be in the tree business and raking it in. Said we'd get the going price, and with the way Christmas trees was going up every year, we'd make a killing. Fine and dandy. It was all just fine and dandy until it came time for him to give me the going price on my half of them trees. Then it's a different story. Tells me three dollars a foot is ridiculous, there's no damn evergreen worth three dollars a foot, and he's not gonna give me that for 'em. Says he'll go two dollars at the most.

Fine, I says. But I'm not signing any right of way to him so he can sell his damn house. His bay window is hanging over my property line, and with the air conditioner stuck in it, it's even farther over the line. Which means he can't sell that old house unless I agree to give him the six feet of easement so the guy at the bank will be happy, and everything will be legal.

You got to wonder how bad he wants to sell the place if he's not willing to give me the price the nurseries are getting for trees that ain't nearly as fresh and pretty as them evergreens. They are as nice a tree as anybody could hope to put up at Christmas, and I got every right to ask the going price.

"They're only half yours," he says. "Actually not even half. All you done is water and trim them some."

"All I done?" I says. "You got any idea how much time and worry I put into getting them sons a bitches to grow straight and bushy, and have a pitcher perfect shape?"

"They did most of that on their own," Kyte says. "Where do you get off thinking you could show an evergreen how to be a tree?"

"That's not what I'm sayin'," I says. "What I'm sayin' is that I kept my half of the bargain, and I got a right to my half of the selling price of them trees, even if I'm selling them to you so you can unload that joke of a house on those poor unsuspecting tenderfoots from Connecticut, who think they're gonna be pioneers or some such shit."

My God, you ought to see these people from Connecticut. The woman's not bad looking, but talk to her for five minutes, and you can tell she don't know a pocket gopher from a screwdriver. And her husband? The guy looks like he's about 6 feet 4 and weighs about 110 pounds. Says he's got some disease where his body is eating itself, so he's got to bicycle all the time to build muscle tissue, and he's all starry-eyed about living in the country and being out here with the badgers and hawks and all the buffalo grass, just like in *Dances with Wolves*, which, as far as I'm concerned, was about as lame-brained as it gets, but that's another subject.

Anyway, these two bookworms are chomping at the bit to spend the $15,000 the woman got from the university over at Vermillion to come there and write plays. I don't know what kind of plays she writes, nor do I give two hoots since I can't stand that kind of stuff—poetry and plays and such like that. But I still feel sheepish when the Connecticut people come around to see the house and walk around the place and talk about being free and getting back to Nature. About the first time the furnace quits, and the windows in that monstrosity start leaking subzero air, they'll be back in Nature all right.

But mainly I hate to see Kyte taking their money without even flinching. But then he's shown his colors on our agreement about the trees, so I'm not surprised he's willing to fleece those tenderfoots so he can buy a house in town and maybe get his wife back.

It almost makes me want to refuse to grant him that right of way just for being so damn greedy and hanging a price on that house at three times what it's worth, with the water problems in the basement and the foundation looking like Swiss cheese and all the window casings crumbling with mold and the wiring chewed to hell by rats and mice and the cesspool backing up about every other month. I used to think Kyte was a decent guy when we were both members of the Dalesburg Baptist Church, but after his wife bolted, he just went to seed. Now all he thinks about is money and the stuff he owns and how he can get more money. He thinks that will bring her back.

He wasn't like that when we first planted the trees, but then he got into this thing where he started buyin' old houses and cleanin' 'em up and sellin' 'em for a big profit. His eyes got beady almost over night and his nose got to looking like the beak of a fuckin' grackle, and then he wasn't Darby Kyte no more. Not the Darby Kyte I knew.

So unless he comes to his senses and gives me my due for them trees, I'm not gonna overlook that air conditioner and the fact that part of his house is hanging over my property. A man has to draw the line somewhere if he wants to respect hisself, and I'm drawing the line on that easement.

● ● ●

Kyte

Mealy-mouthed little weasel, Earl Fitch. If he thinks he can put the squeeze on me and rip me off just because he watered some trees on my land, he's in for a surprise. Those trees were my idea in the first place, and it was my water he used to raise them up to where they are right now, and my tools he used to prune and fuss with them. So damned if I'll give him some outrageous price to buy his half out. He's not even entitled to half as far as I'm concerned, but then I'm a man of my word, and I'm not about to renege on a deal once I've shook hands on it.

The thing is he's gone and inflated the price now that he's got me in a pinch with the sale of my house hanging in the balance. What kind of friend is that? The little weasel. It was just good business. Just like I'm doing with the people from Connecticut who want to buy my place.

It's their dream come true, and who am I to rain on their parade? You can see it in their eyes how much they like the place and how excited they are to get it. The little lowlife blackmailing me after I told him about that place next door being for sale, with the Gustafsons getting a divorce and all, and their son going off to jail for piping child porn into his computer, and their daughter getting in a car wreck so all she can do is sit in a chair at the rest home and stare at the wall. It wasn't nothing wrong with telling Fitch to lowball them on the price, they were desperate, and that's what he did. They been telling people in town that Fitch stole the place from them, but it was fair and square. Easterners just love it out here with all this space because there's no space left back east, so they're in pig heaven when they can get out in the open and see nothing but sky and corn fields and soaring hawks and a big red sun on the horizon. I told them how peaceful and private the place is before they ever saw it, and once they saw it, they said it was just like I said, just like being in the Garden of Eden. Course calling South Dakota the Garden of Eden is quite a stretch in my mind, but then we're not talking about me. If they want to call it Eden and call each other Adam and Eve, that's fine with me, just as long as they sign the papers.

So if that damn Fitch will just cooperate, everyone will get what they want. But then it's hard to say what Fitch will do next. He says he never knew about that part of my house bein' on his land, but I think he knew it all along, and was just waiting for a chance to stab me in the back.

I used to think he was a humble man, a God-fearing man, who was OK with living a simple life. But now it comes out he's no different than the rest of the damn country, thinking they need to be living the high life. He wasn't in that house six months, and he was buying fancy furniture and television sets and a new truck, all on Dale's electronics wages. Just going kind of nuts, the way my son, Corbin, and his wife have done down in Omaha. Living the life of Reilly down there in the suburbs, with their two kids, their snowmobiles, their hot tub, their three-car garage, their boat, their Jet Skis, their satellite dish, their Dalmation, and their big screen TV. I don't begrudge them any of it, but I know for a fact that most of it's not paid for, and I have to bite my tongue when Corbin starts telling me that I'm out of date and better get into the twentieth century before it ends. I don't say anything, just change the subject or pick up a football and tell one of the boys to go out for a pass. A couple of times I've been pissed off enough to tell Kayleen that I'm not going back down there for any more visits, especially holidays when I have to listen to their version of *The Price Is Right* for two or three days. Kayleen always talked me out of getting riled up, said it was just the generation gap, which is probably true, but there's been many a night I've lain awake, wondering what will happen to them if there's any layoffs at that computer company, and they're suddenly out of a job. Damn computer companies are the closest thing we've got to the gold rush days in the Old West. Boom and bust, and everything riding on fantasy and greed. Spooky as can be. But I don't say anything to Corbin because he's got the same attitude so many of these chipheads have—the future is just one big piece of cheese and they've got a power-driven slicer.

That's how Fitch got—like he had a power slicer and free access to the cheese. He went out and got him a leggy, frizz-haired barmaid ten years younger than him, who works over at Clayton's on the River, and set up house with her. It wasn't a month before she had him filling that house with lamps and chairs and TVs and dining room sets, and him trying to do it all on Dale's electronics wages. Which meant he had to work sixty-hour weeks to keep up with the bills; so he was never home, and neither was she. So he comes home one night from an over-time shift, and no sign of her. He jumps in his truck and drives across the bridge into Nebraska, heading for Clayton's.

The front door of Clayton's is locked when he gets there. All the dining room and parking lot lights are out, and there's no sign of anyone being around, but he thinks he hears voices somewhere toward the rear of the building. He decides he'll see what he can see around the back. Takes him a while to creep through the bushes and trees and walk the top of the ballast without falling in the river, but he finally gets around to the back of the building and spots a lighted window on the far side. Told me later that he wished he'd never looked in that window because one of the bartenders was layin' the timber to his little chickadee up on a pool table. Said her legs were wrapped around the big lunk's back, and he could hear both of them gasping and yelping, and billiard balls bouncing off the table onto the floor, and the brass lamp above them swaying like it was going to come loose any second.

That was the end of Fitch's house dolly, and it wasn't long before he'd sold all that stuff he'd bought to impress her and went back to living the simple life he had when I met him. He had some acres of bottomland the other side of his place, and come spring he planted corn in there, and that seemed to take his mind off what he'd seen that night at Clayton's.

He was going along just fine until this thing came up about the easement, then all of a sudden he's back to being a mealy-mouthed little coyote, like to bite you soon as look at you. I don't know what to make of it, except plain old jealousy over me fixing up all my places in town and making a good profit on them. I don't see what his gripe is when he could do the same thing. Problem with him, though, is he's gotten tighter than the skin on a wet drum after that fiasco with the barmaid, and he talks about doing stuff, but he won't part with the cash. He works his ass off more than ever doing overtime at Dale's, and just squirrels the money in the bank, which is another reason I don't understand why he's being such an asshole about the easement and the trees.

Well, I'm not beat yet. I'll figure something out, some way to get him to sign those papers so I can give the people from Connecticut a chance at their dream. I'll never get Kayleen back if I don't have a place out at that Pheasant Run development. I don't know if I can live next door to a bunch of counter hoppers from town, but I'm willing to give it a try if it means Kayleen will come to her senses and come home. That's why I can't let Earl Fitch ruin my plans.

● ● ●

Fitch

I don't know why I gave in to that needle nose Kyte. He looks like a grackle more every day. His eyes have got beadier than ever, just like he's turning into a grackle, which are the meanest, most cold-hearted birds around. Watch them some time out on a lawn. They don't let no other birds share the beetles or worms. They chase them off and peck the shit out of them; then they go strutting around, darting their nasty little yellow eyes around like they own the world. The more money Kyte made, the more he acted like that, to where I figured he'd never see things my way on the trees. But just when you think you've got someone figured out, they pull the rug on you.

So I gave him his easement. Don't know if I did it because he offered $2.50 a foot for the trees, or because it was so damn pathetic to see an old fishin' and huntin' buddy whining and sniffling about getting his wife back. Funny how you feel sorry for someone you'd like to push in the river, but then the whole thing was starting to get on my nerves to where I couldn't sleep at night, worryin' about what he might pull to get me to sign. I need my sleep, and I like the way things are going at work, so I just figured good riddance.

Sure enough, soon as he got that place sold to the people from Connecticut, he went into town and bought a big fancy house out there at Pheasant Run across from the state loony bin. The way I figure it, he won't have far to walk when his wife starts gambling again. I suppose everyone deserves a second chance, but the way I see it, you can paint the stripes on a skunk black, but it's still a skunk. I've seen way too many people hooked on that gambling since they voted it in. It makes them just plain crazy. Good people you'd never think would steal from their employers and stuff like that to cover their losses.

That's how Kyte's wife was doing. She was spending her paycheck and most of his, and jumpin' banks and gettin' new credit cards until she was in about $80,000. Then when the creditors started sniffin' her out, she blew town. Left old Kyte holding the bag. He had to scramble like hell to pay all the bills off, and didn't even know where she'd gone. Then one morning out of the blue he gets a letter telling him she's living with some French Canadian hockey player up in the Twin Cities and wants a divorce. Kyte was so damn worried about her he forgot to get mad, but he had enough gumption to tell her to get her ass home, he wasn't giving her no divorce. Then he felt like shit for two weeks after he did that, so he got her phone number and called her and begged her to come back, and what would it take for her to do it? That's when she laid it on him about a house in town and going out to dinner at the Black Angus and such if she came back. He never said so, but I got the feeling he promised her the damn moon if she'd get on an airplane and fly to Sioux Falls.

I think he regretted going to jelly so fast because a few weeks later the hockey player gave Kayleen a black eye and busted one of her wrists, and she was on that airplane in a flash. Kyte was still in the house next to me at the time, but he had to be out of there in ten days so the people from Connecticut could move in. He told me he was supposed to fumigate the place for roaches and termites as part of the deal, but he didn't have no time for it, so would I keep it to myself about him not fumigating. I figured those tenderfoots wouldn't notice the roaches, or maybe they'd decide it would be real big-hearted to let the roaches come in and keep warm for the winter.

Soon as Kyte was gone, they moved in. The husband got a job in the bike shop at Ace Hardware in Yankton, and the wife went off to write her plays at the university. I never seen much of them on through the fall, but one day in mid-January she came over to ask if she could borrow a flashlight since they'd had their electricity shut off for getting behind on the bill. That's when she sat in my kitchen huddled by the stove and sipping the coffee I gave her with a shot of Old Crow in it and told me they were in one hell of a fix. They'd defaulted on their loan in November and December after the bean pole got fired for missing work because of his sickness and because he couldn't ride his bicycle into Yankton on the cold days. So then he'd turned their van into a traveling bike shop and painted THE BIKE DOCTOR on the side and started going around the countryside, fixing bicycles and tricycles.

I guess it went OK until the German shepherd they bought to have out on the land with them attacked some farmer's poodle right in the front yard and killed it. That was the end of the Bike Doctor. Then the bean pole got even sicker and needed more medicine, and the wife's stipend couldn't cover everything. Then the furnace screeched to a halt one night, and they'd had to chop firewood to stay warm. They were sending for money and would catch up soon. "We're about to turn a corner," she kept saying, and I just nodded. She said she was going to start waitressing at Smith's Pool Hall in Yankton to help them get on through to spring. I gave her the flashlight and some extra batteries and told her good luck. For a minute after she left, I was thinking what a snake Darby Kyte was for selling them that house, but then, as P.T. Barnum once said, "There's a sucker born every minute," and what are you gonna do?

Two months later they turned a corner all right, at the junction of Highway 50 and Interstate 90 East on their way back to Connecticut. It wasn't a month before the bank had someone renting the place until they found some way to unload it. Near as I can tell, it's a bunch of twenty somethings, mostly riff-raff from town, and the rumor I heard at Toby's Lounge in Meckling is that they're dealing drugs out of there, or maybe even got a meth lab going. There's more of those labs popping up around here, so I wouldn't be surprised. Especially with the way so damn many cars come and go and don't ever stay more than a half hour. There hasn't been that much traffic on Timber Road since I been out here, and now I'm wishing I'd sold when Kyte did.

● ● ●

Kyte
I saw Fitch at Toby's in Meckling a couple weeks back, and I guess he's got his place up for sale. The people I sold to are long gone, and now he thinks there's a bunch of pot-heads living in that beautiful old house. If I'd a known that was going to happen, I'd never sold. That house was more or less a fixer-upper, but it had all kinds of potential. Before Kayleen started gambling, we had plans to restore it to being the beautiful mansion it was back in the early days of Dakota Territory. Those old places had a splendor you don't see any more. It's a damn shame. But I did what I had to. I got Kayleen back, and she's staying out of the casinos. She's drinking a lot, but I'll take that over the gambling.

I was out in the country looking at a run-down house for sale, so I decided to stop by Fitch's place. He was out checking his corn patch, said it was going be his best crop ever. The only problem was he'd sold his house to some young couple from Vermillion, who were driving him crazy to take possession of the house. Just a couple spoiled kids like so many of what you see nowadays—real pushy and want everything right now. Which is why they didn't want to listen to the loan guy at the bank, who told them they couldn't take possession until Fitch harvested that corn. Fitch figured they could damn well wait one month to get in there even if they had ordered carpet and given up the place they were renting in Vermillion.

"What the hell do they think they're doing ordering carpet to be put in out here next week?" Fitch says. "Are they mental or what?"

"Hold your ground," I says. "There's probably a hang-up on the loan with that corn in the picture. Besides, you've got some money coming from the looks of that crop."

"Damn right I do," Fitch says, and he got that look in his eyes like he had when he set his jaw about the evergreens. I knew they wouldn't get him out of there until he was ready.

As it turned out, he got the bank to delay the loan so he could harvest the corn, which he did. But in the meantime, the basement flooded and ruined the carpet those little punks had installed while he was down in Council Bluffs at a funeral, and Fitch got stuck with the flood bill. When I heard that he was in a lurch, I took some big fans out there and an industrial shop vac, and we sucked the place dry and set the fans going. Fitch was still in the dumps, but I told him about a place I'd seen over by Wakonda, and told him I'd help him get it.

● ● ●

Fitch

Some friend that Earl Kyte is. That guy is a real prince. He put me on to the place I'm in now, and it's got all kinds of good acreage and a crik running through and like that. The house is twice as big as the old place and is in bad shape, but Kyte says he'll help me fix it up.

Then on top of that, we're gonna plant twice as many evergreens on a big flat south of the house, and we're gonna raise bird dogs. Kyte says there's money to be made in bird dogs with the way pheasant hunting is exploding in the state. I can't wait to get the kennels built and start raising them dogs. Kyte says I'll be good at it because I'm good with animals, and I believe him. He's always been a good neighbor. And if you can't trust your neighbors, who can you trust?

The Fallen

THEY BURIED CHARLOTTE SMITH'S SON, Jarrod, a nineteen-year-old private in the US Army, on a crisp October morning in the Black Hills National Cemetery between Spearfish and Sturgis. Jarrod had been killed by a roadside bomb on September 26, a few miles west of Baghdad, and it had taken a week just to get his body back to Sundance, Wyoming, where he had grown up and where his mother, a thin, bandy-legged waitress at the Arc Light Café had lived all of her forty-eight years. The day had been so yellow and orange under a throbbing blue sky that it seemed to Charlotte at the time like a day no one could die. She realized at the graveside while the minister was conducting funeral rites that this was not the day Jarrod had died, but another day, a day of tribute and honor and patriotic glory.

At least it seemed so at the time, but over the winter, every time she glanced at her son's photo mounted in a place of honor between two small American flags on the north wall of the Arc Light's dining room, she felt the glory fading. In place of the feelings of pride and purpose she had experienced in her deeply wounded heart when hearing all the wonderful things that both civilians and military officials said about Jarrod at the wake and funeral, there was a nagging voice, an actual voice that hung in her memory from the funeral. On the way back to the mortuary limousine, with the cemetery crowd fragmenting and dispersing in the fresh, fiery reaches of an Indian Summer day, she heard a man's voice, a voice she didn't recognize, mutter to another mourner, "It better be worth it."

Try as she might to drive the comment from her mind over the next eight months, counter it with all the sentiments and words of encouragement, the prayer cards, the phone calls, the boxes of Jarrod's childhood photographs, the expense-paid trip she'd made to Washington, DC, for a weekend with parents of other fallen soldiers, the question only grew larger, more insistent. They'd killed her son, her only child. They'd recruited him into the army and sent him off to Iraq to be killed. In many respects, she still clung to the things the army officers said at the funeral, the things her friends and neighbors said, the condolences and words of gratitude offered to her by customers at the Arc Light Café. Jarrod was a hero protecting his country. He died so that we could all go on with our way of life. Our way of life . . . our way of life.

But there were still times when reading the newspaper or watching the daily news on television with all its vulgar, disgusting stories, its political scandals, its tales of greed and cruelty, its relentless tally and talk of bombings in Iraq, she felt a void opening inside her, a black cavern in which echoed that voice, "It better be worth it."

Though she shared the inner turbulence with no one, losing herself in the grind and grease, the come and go of the Arc Light Café—ribbing the cooks and bussers, joking with customers, sneaking a smoke in the alley during a lull—she had her moments of doubt. They lodged in her mind and surfaced without warning, and she'd have to face down the demon while walking home from work or sitting in the bathtub trying to coax the pain out of her ankles and back with the hottest water she could stand. Sometimes she drove the demon off, felt the knot leave her diaphragm, the heavy stone roll off her mind. Other times the temptation to see Jarrod's death as a waste, a mockery, a terrible crime committed by the government against a single mother and a naive boy, gripped her mind and heart like the jaws of a snapping turtle that had seized her ankle as a little girl, and it was all she could do to hold the hatred and bitterness back.

With Jarrod's $200,000 military death benefit sitting in a bank in Rapid City, she sometimes thought she should just walk away from the Arc Light job, pay off her house, and go see the world. But every time she considered spending any of what she couldn't help but think of as blood money, it felt like she'd be killing Jarrod a second time; so until she could come to a point of seeing and feeling differently about that money, she hung onto the hit-and-miss comfort of her life as a waitress.

By summer the visitations of doubt had become more frequent and unpredictable, though she noticed that the blackness often came when she was fatigued, beat, a walking zombie. Like tonight, a hot dry Monday evening in mid-August, the dining room emptying out and only one hour to close. She was bent over, washing and straightening a table, her back aching and her shoulder muscles burning from all the trays she'd been toting during a huge rush of bikers heading west, the motor cycle rally in Sturgis having ended the day before. She glanced at her watch to note one hour to go, then happened to look up at her son's photograph on the wall above the table and had to turn away quickly because of the sudden urge she had to sink to her knees and start screaming obscenities.

The day, the past weeks had worn her emotions threadbare, pounded her to a pulp with the roaring Harley frenzy of Sundance in the summer, strangers pouring through the town from West Virginia, Massachusetts, Ohio, Alabama, and Minnesota, ripping off big pieces of the American Dream, gulping down the sky, flying through the Badlands in a fury of food and drink and sex and trinkets and tee shirts, wallowing in their free country freedom like there was no tomorrow. They tore across South Dakota and invaded the West like the first waves of settlers and cowboys and saloon girls, seeing and not seeing the gas station attendants, the motel desk clerks, the fast food counter help, the waitresses like Charlotte, hurrying to set their feasts before them.

She hurried to the employee's rest room to gather herself, to tuck her sudden sense of invisibility and nothingness behind her ears with the long shocks of streaked blonde hair. Staring at herself in the mirror, she saw how frazzled she looked, how beat; so she threw some water on her face, straightened the lapels on her blouse, and thought suddenly of the Easter morning Jarrod had left a white azalea on the dining room table for her. Its white blossoms loomed in her mind's eye, lifted her away from the urge to walk through the dining room and out of the Arc Light Café and not look back.

She questioned her decision to finish her shift a few minutes later when she approached a table where a middle-aged woman and a young woman were waiting. The older woman, whom Charlotte pegged quickly as the mother, immediately began a patter of disclaimer and explanation about her daughter being a vegan.

"I see," Charlotte said. "Well, there are some of the Mexican entrees that don't have meat."

"I'm strictly vegan," the college-age girl said, raising a sour, sober face. "I have far more restrictions than most people who claim to be vegetarian. It's almost impossible for me to find anything to eat in the Midwest."

"Well, I . . ."

"Is there any lard in the vegetable medley?"

"I'd say no," Charlotte said, her poise kicking in. "But I'd be happy to check for you."

"She has to be sure," the mother said. "She takes this very seriously."

"I'm sure she does," Charlotte said. "That dinner comes in a frozen bag; I'll go read the ingredients."

"Bring me the bag," the girl said, her expression remaining cool and distant.

"I can do that," Charlotte said. "Be right back."

In the kitchen she asked Ronnie, the cook, where he kept the bags of frozen vegetables.

"Second freezer, down low," he said. "What's the problem?"

"Got a vegan out there wants to see if there's any lard in the medley."

"Oh for Christ's sake, just tell her there ain't no lard. Fuckin' people anyway."

Charlotte found the vegetables, carried the bag out into the smoky, greasy light of the kitchen, and quickly read the list of ingredients.

"Be back in a minute," she told Ronnie.

She carried the bag out to the dining room and handed it to the young woman. "No lard."

The young woman clutched the bag of vegetables like an eagle grasping a salmon and studied the back, running her index finger slowly down the bag.

"I knew it," she said. "There. Right there. Lard!"

"I'm sorry," Charlotte said. "I didn't see it."

"Perhaps another entrée, dear?" the mother said. "Don't give up, darling."

The young woman was frowning more noticeably now and tapping one of her sandaled feet on the tile.

"As usual I have to make something up," she said. "This burrito supreme?"

"Yes?"

"Can you have them leave the meat out and put in mushrooms?"

"Mushrooms?"

"Yes, mushrooms. For the protein. I haven't had any protein today. Just make sure that there are lots of mushrooms in there. And no meat."

"No problem," Charlotte said, turning to the mother. "And for you?'

"I'll have the tuna salad, please."

"And to drink?'

"We'll both have the raspberry iced tea," the mother said.

Charlotte finished writing on her pad, slid it in her apron pocket, and hurried away.

"Fine," Ronnie said when she gave him the order. "The candy-ass gets her mushrooms."

"It's OK, Ronnie. She has a right to order what she wants. Just no burger, OK?"

Charlotte went back out to the dining room and took orders from a young couple with two young sons, and from an older couple, the only remaining customers. She hung the orders on the chrome wheel glinting in the kitchen's cubby hole window, then entered the kitchen to prepare the glasses of iced tea while she waited for Ronnie to finish the orders for the two women.

"Where do they get this shit?" she heard Ronnie mutter to himself. "It's fucking Wyoming!"

It looked to Charlotte as though Ronnie had met the demands of the order, so she delivered it to the table, sucking a smile from her diminishing reserves. Neither of the two women looked up or said anything. She glanced around the room to see that no new customers had come in, and then returned to the kitchen to get the appetizers for the young couple and their two bashful sons. Such simple, nondescript families, who were clearly on a tight budget and wonderfully humble about it, were among her favorite customers, and their presence seemed to offset the cranky, demanding diners.

She had just set a bread basket on the young couple's table and was on her way to the fountain for some glasses of ice water they had chosen for beverages when the college girl waved her over to the table. The girl had unfolded the burrito and scattered its contents around the plate.

"That," she said, pointing her fork at a gray lump on the plate, "is a piece of meat."

"No, ma'am, it's a mushroom. I'm sure."

"This," she said, pointing her fork at another gray lump, "is a mushroom. That thing is hamburger, and it touched all the other stuff."

"The juices, you understand," the mother said. "The whole burrito is contaminated with meat juices."

"I could get you another one, I could . . ."

"I'll just eat the beans and rice."

"But I can . . ."

"Never mind. Just take it away."

"Here," Charlotte said, her voice quaking. "Use this plate for the beans and rice. I'll take the burrito. And I'll adjust your bill."

She held her temper until she reached the garbage disposal in the kitchen, then picked the burrito off the plate and flung it down the hole. Then she sat down on a stool by the bread oven and started to cry. Ronnie came over and put a bacon-smelling hand on her shoulder.

"What kind of bullshit people do we got in this country anyway?" he said. "So goddamned spoiled it ain't funny, and the rest of us bustin' our balls so's they can run around and act like assholes."

He paused, patting Charlotte's shoulder.

"Good thing you got class, Charlotte. If it was me, she'd a got that burrito in the kisser. Fact, if you want, I'll go out there and tell her what I think of her right now."

Charlotte stood up and dried her tears on her apron.

"We've only got twenty-five minutes to closing, Ronnie. Let's not make any trouble. It'll be OK. I just need to go home and lie down."

"Gotcha," Ronnie said. "You workin' late again tomorrow?"

"Yes, I am."

"Good. Then you can sleep in."

"I plan on it."

• • •

Half an hour after closing, Charlotte came out the side door of the Arc Light and walked around the building to the front sidewalk. She crossed the street and headed east, past the rows of motels on that side—Budget Host, The Lamplighter, Sun Dance Motel—all full. When she came to the Bear Lodge Motel, she stopped to look through the front window at the night-time lobby. Old Lyle Bellman ran a tight ship, loved being in the motel business, had spent the last twenty-five years running Bear Lodge. He was kind of a strange old guy that she thought might be a Holy Roller, but she admired the way he kept his place, had heard many of his customers comment on the upkeep and cleanliness of his rooms.

She peered around the lobby at the heavy leather furniture and rough wood coffee tables and up at the deer and elk heads jutting from the walls, the cream-colored tips of their antlers curving into the darkness of the ceiling. She smiled at the thought of all the hunters who came through Sundance, many of them from the big cities and excited to be out in the mountains of Wyoming, hunting deer and elk. They were generous, spirited men, and were some of her best-tipping customers. Looking up at the eerie beauty of the heads, she could sense the source of their excitement, the unfettered magic and freedom of stalking such creatures in the woods.

She turned from the window and walked a few steps before taking a sharp right under the stonework arch over the entrance to the motel units and crossed the courtyard as a shortcut to her house a few streets over. Every parking spot was filled with pick-ups, SUVs, and motorcycles. She could see the deep metallic gleam and flash of seven or eight Harley Davidsons nosed up to the sidewalk on the right side.

Charlotte loved to look at the bikes up close, so she veered over that direction. She stopped to admire the first two pairs of bikes, careful not to touch them, standing there imagining coming around a curve in the Black Hills sitting behind the husband she'd lost to an oil rig accident near Gillette almost twenty years ago. It was something they had talked about a lot before Jarrod was born and were still hoping to do when Tom was killed. She stepped around the bikes and moved toward the last one parked in front of the last unit near the alley. She stopped to look more closely, not realizing the door to the room was partially open. When she glanced up, she saw a bearded, bare-chested man in jeans and a black leather vest sitting on the bed with a bottle of whiskey in his hand while a voluptuous peroxide-blonde woman wearing only an elk tooth necklace danced provocatively to some music blaring from speakers at the rear of the room.

Charlotte was transfixed for a moment as the muted red and orange lights of the room crossed and re-crossed the woman's deeply tanned body. Then she turned and hurried down the dim alley, head lowered, eyes fixed on the gravel-strewn path.

● ● ●

At home, her feet covered to the ankles in scalding water, she felt the evening rise up from her ankles to her torso and shoulders and then lift away. Her thoughts leaned momentarily, like a sapling in a breeze, toward the nagging desire to match the loss of her son with what she encountered daily at the Arc Light Café as our way of life, our freedom—the truckers, the hunters, the young couple taking their sons on a meager vacation, the grouchy young vegan, the biker and his naked playmate. She had no mind for fitting it all together in a sealed package that could be tied with a bow, but she knew that people and their stations in life were and were not the "thing" Jarrod had died for. So she pulled back from the echoing refrain of "It better be worth it," not caring whether it was or wasn't. As near as she could tell, the answer, if there was one, was lost along with Jarrod. She thought instead about what Jarrod had said about it all, about what America meant to him and why he felt compelled to enlist.

For Jarrod, it was not about people so much as about an idea, his faith in a beautiful idea. And Jarrod's faith was good enough for her. It buoyed her up and urged her forward like the water that was relaxing her feet and legs, giving her the means to get up tomorrow morning and go on.

Girl on a Float

YOU ARE SEVENTEEN, AND YOU are riding atop a homecoming float in a low-cut lavender dress, which leaves your shoulders and a good portion of your chest turning reddish pink, even purple in spots from the chill of a sleet-spitting October afternoon in Wall, South Dakota, where the prairie fans every direction toward a flat, welded seam of land and horizon. You are shivering between smiles and hand waves to the people gathered along Dennison Avenue, just a block behind Wall's Main Street, and you are thrilled to be homecoming queen, which is something you've dreamed about since you were six. So even though the day—which started mild and sunny—has turned gray with cloud cover and cold in the rising wind and dust, your entourage travels the parade route to the cheers of small crowds gathered on street corners and lawns, on the sidewalks of nondescript streets adjacent to the Wall Drug corridor with its gift and jewelry shops, lounges and casinos, where, on this mid-October day second-wave tourists are drifting and dawdling.

At various places along the way, you catch a glimpse of your tiara in a store or car window, its gold points rising like your deepest hopes into the subtle drift of Badlands clouds.

The image of the float carrying you and your five-girl court, the lucky-duck royalty of this 1995 Wall High School Homecoming is like a magic boat in a stark sienna sea, and the weight of your crown and its golden gleam helps you ward off the chill in the air, ignore the ache in your back from sitting so long on a crepe-covered sawhorse. And it helps you tough out the grit and the icy drops of rain pelting your forehead and unraveling the beautiful bouffant you spent $25 on, using up what was left of your Dairy Queen money from the summer and not regretting it at all because it was the hairstyle you'd been dreaming of all summer, every time you fantasized about winning Homecoming Queen.

You keep tucking strands of hair in place, trying to angle your head below the gusts of wind that come whipping into intersections or between buildings, so you strain to look royal and stately for the crowd, and smile and wave and smile and wave, fingertips going numb in the faux-diamond-trimmed gloves that cover at least part of your arms to the elbow. Your biceps and shoulders are starting to sting in spots, go numb in others, and the chill between your breasts seems to be working down around your ribs and thighs, which are starting to burn with cold beneath the petticoats and layers of lavender chiffon.

Once you pass the business district, you notice the girls in your court, sitting in a semi-circle two tiers down on the float, pulling throws and shawls from under their seats and huddling under them as the float jounces up the slope through the last residential neighborhood, and, rounding a bend, begins its ascent to the high school. You wish you had brought a shawl or sweater along, but the weather forecast had said mild and sunny, high in the low fifties, and besides, you are the queen, and people want to see you there at the top of the float, a symbol of beauty and victory. It's your job to set an example, to show the school spirit that got you elected Homecoming Queen.

So you suck it up, ride with your neck and face burning, and try your best to be a good sport. That's what it's all about, isn't it? Being a good sport, caring about others? That was all they talked about at Girls' State in Vermillion last summer, and you were inspired by everything you saw and heard there, you were determined to set an example, to put those ideals into action, to make your senior year a living tribute to leadership. Then, if you could score well enough on the ACT, you would go to the University of South Dakota and major in political science, with a specialization in international relations. After that, the sky would be the limit, as Ms. Crawford, your volleyball coach, would say, so you're not going to be defeated by a little temporary discomfort on a float.

In the distance, the land sweeps west to the Black Hills and east to the Badlands, and the sky arcs in autumn tints, clouds feathered above the towering tin grain elevator bins at the far end of Main Street. You can see the black gouges of gulches and draws, the silhouettes of leafless trees on the ridges, in the ravines, as the caravan climbs toward the high school parking lot.

Your teeth are chattering and your stomach is knotted from holding onto yourself, but you ride with queenly pride, rise above the stinging slap of wind, and think about the dance tonight and your date with Ross Rogers, the star running back for the undefeated Wall Eagles. You see yourself dancing in his arms, can't believe how handsome he is when your eyes meet. You can't believe this has happened to you, Vivian Walsh, that he's asked you to the dance after two years of sneaking glances at him over the tops of history and geometry books, or catching his eye at assemblies or in the lunchroom, and having him give you the smile that melts you like butter on a hot stove. This will be the night you've dreamed of since starting high school, and if all goes well, the beginning of a romance with Ross Rogers.

So you buck up, face into the wind, and press your tiara like a set of gilded antlers into the sprawling expanse of your future.

● ● ●

The homecoming dance flares out beyond all expectation. Afterwards, in Ross Rogers's Mustang convertible beneath some big cottonwood trees on an old farm road, engine running, heater on high, CD crooning in the background, you let Ross Rogers kiss you long and hard and then kiss you some more. You let him touch you wherever he wants, let him unzip the back of your formal and slide it off your shoulders. Let him kiss his way down your chest while you slide the rest of the way out of the dress. He is out of his clothes like he's breaking into the secondary for an eighty-yard touchdown run, and the night swirls down to a rhythmic yin and yang—his ruthless grunts, your ecstatic gasps.

By April, you are two months pregnant. Your emotions are all over the map—fear, joy, amazement, curiosity—but, most of all, excitement at the thought of spending the rest of your life with Ross Rogers. That dream dominates your thoughts day and night until you finally get the right moment to tell Ross the news. When the first thing Ross says is that his dad will pay half the cost of the abortion, you look out the window of the Prairie Winds Café and up the weed-covered slope at the cement dinosaur standing on the ridge above the freeway, and you know it's the beginning of the end of you and Ross Rogers.

By May, Ross has a new girlfriend—Daisy Kolstad—and word is that, come August, they are heading for Spearfish where Ross will play football for the Black Hills State Yellow Jackets.

You think you've seen the worst of it, secretly hoping that Ross will tire of Daisy, who is the biggest flirt in western South Dakota, and that he will call some night and ask you to come to Spearfish with him, just the three of you—him, you, and the baby. When he and Daisy, partying late on a scorching July night and going the wrong way down the freeway, drive the Mustang under an eighteen-wheeler, and Ross is decapitated, you are horribly shaken, can't believe he's dead. You're shaken again when you go to the hospital to wish Daisy well and see her lying in a speechless stupor, eyes riveted on a seashell mobile while drool runs from the corners of her mouth.

You're embarrassingly glad it wasn't you in the car with Ross. You think about Daisy all the time, see her in your mind's eye lying comatose beneath the dangling shells, see her blank, eternal stare even when you are deep in the throes of childbirth. The contractions crack your body open and your life surges forth into the days and weeks and months you've spent glancing at the freshly painted totem pole above the entrance to Wall Drug, where you sell Black Hills gold jewelry to people from Texas and New Jersey and Illinois—a steady stream of faces that runs together into a single Tourist Face.

The mega-face merges with the faces on the totem pole, which, mounted on the lip of the ratty gray shakes covering the awning, stares toward the bentonite plant where your husband, Cody, one of Ross Rogers's front line blockers, works nights so he can care for your two children during the day—the girl Ross wanted to abort and the boy you and Cody made together in the sulfur-smelling heat of your trailer house north of Wall. And you sell Black Hills gold rings, earrings, bracelets, belt buckles, and watches. Waves of bikers and parrot-voiced tourists shuffle through the log wall catacombs of Wall Drug, staring at stuffed jackalopes and photos of dead Indians, touching whiskey jiggers and key chains and carnival glass gophers, babbling about ice cream cones and Wild Bill Hickock, and whispering about the sheet-metal poster with the buckskin-clad Indian maiden riding a buffalo, one breast bared, eyes searching the heavens for a sign that the Ghost Dance is going to work.

The faces come and the faces go, and the sun beats down on the totem pole, the visages of crow and hawk, eagle and owl bleaching, splitting, tiny shards of paint flaking off in the long flow of August afternoons, November afternoons, April afternoons. The seasons roll one into another until it seems like Fall is but one day of yellow leaves blowing down the street, Spring is just a passing echo of geese cries. And then it's summer again, sweltering, choked with dust and the fumes of motorcycle exhaust, the roar of engines, and the endless waves of bikers with their tattoos and their leathered faces.

And you're still standing behind the three-sided glass counter, coonskin caps and fox fur pelts dangling from a rafter overhead. Gold necklaces, gold pendants, gold bracelets, gold lapel pins gleam on the black velvet as you bend and lift and open and close and explain and encourage. Your knees are barely able to bend, and you're only twenty-five years old, already seven years out of high school—where did it go?— and now your two oldest children are in kindergarten and first grade, and there's a toddler at home.

So hard to make ends meet after Cody gets laid off at the bentonite plant for almost eight months, and you have to take a second job waiting tables at the Coyote Club across the street. Which is a madhouse from April to September with the new casino they've added, and you have to wear a revealing outfit that has you worried your breasts will fall out some night while you're setting a steak on the table. And the black spike heels and the fishnet stockings; so embarrassing even though you still have something of the figure you had in high school, except for the wider hips. In time you manage to get used to the outfit and to let the things men say to you slide off, along with the pats on the butt and the unabashed ogling of your breasts. It's all a blur, like your mornings at home, like tending to the children's needs and keeping your husband's hopes up until they finally call him back to work.

Now you are faced with not having anyone to watch the kids in the evenings while you race around the Coyote Club, catching a glimpse of yourself in the mirror behind the bar or in the chrome border of the cigarette machine, and your mind darts suddenly, inexplicably to that October afternoon you rode a Kleenex castle through the streets of Wall.

You cobble together a babysitting exchange with the next-door neighbor whose husband has left her for a lady biker, but the child care exchange lasts only two months because Jocelyn, the neighbor woman, decides to move to Rapid City to sell real estate.

"It's booming there," she keeps telling you. "I'm going to make a killing."

By the time Jocelyn leaves for the promised land, you are grateful you don't have to hear any more about the housing boom in Rapid City, which, from what you've seen the few times you've been there the last couple years, is just more ugly suburban sprawl and desecration of a beautiful place the US Government stole from the Indians. You don't say this to anyone, especially Nick DeRoche, your boss at the Coyote Club, since he thinks of himself as one of the rich and famous of Wall and is always talking about his trips to Denver with the Duprees and the Hemsteads, who own Wall Drug. You were told he was a womanizer when you took the job there, but you ignored the remark because you needed the money. Then one night just after closing he sends a busser to tell you he'd like to see you in his office. You're not in his office five minutes before he is telling you how sweet your legs are, what a beautiful mouth you have, and in a couple more conversational

leaps, asks you to suck the penis he pulls from the zipper of his
frontier pants.

That incident solves your babysitting problem, and you
slide back into the old one-job routine at the Wall Drug Trading Post. The months roll on, the years collapse like an accor-
dion squeezed, like a single year stuck on PAUSE, even though
you're eight years into the new millennium. But there seems
no newness in your life until an explosion at the bentonite
plant takes one of Cody's legs off at the knee, and you are suddenly the main breadwinner for two adults and three children,
one of them in her last year of middle school—a beautiful,
over-sexed girl, who is the spitting image of Ross Rogers. She
is wild as a March hare and gives you fits with her loud music and outrageous taste in clothing and cosmetics. But she's
shown no interest in or symptoms of drug or alcohol abuse
yet, and so far you've been able to limit her dating with midnight curfews and the frequent care of the two younger children while you take on another job at Legacy Old Time Photo.

Legacy Old Time Photo is a retro pioneer photo shop
where, for fifteen hours a week, you are surrounded by a pho-
tographic history of Dakota Territory—small, weather-beat-
en people gathered in front of corrals or near the entrances
to sod houses; sober, hard-bitten cowhands crouching by a
campfire. And the photos you can't quit looking at when the
store isn't busy—the nineteenth-century women of the prairie, their real faces furtive under stoic masks, eyes squinted
to slits in the sweltering sun, jaws clenched, hands curled into
fists as they stand awkwardly in front of prairie schooners or
general stores, buttoned to the neck in drab dresses and shoes,
bonnets removed and hair drawn tight in rigid censure of
their dreams.

Through the front window of Legacy Old Time Photo, in
the dwindling light of summer, fall, winter, spring, summer,

fall, spring, winter, summer, winter, fall, summer, winter you see across the street the totem pole rising above the boardwalk awning of the Wall Drug Trading Post. Its bird faces falter with age and the blister of Badlands wind, the scorch of prairie sun, the harsh piranha bite of sleet and snow. The original glow of head and beak, the cobalt sneer of the crow, the eyes of the owl, the eagle's wind-ruffled mane are streaked in driftwood gray, like displaced idols washed to the shores of an inland sea when the glaciers receded and the dinosaurs and the mastodons vanished in the muck. The totem pole holds steady in the wind, a tower of heads facing the sweep of burnt fields, the grinding white glare of sky.

Seldom do you look up at the totem pole in the early morning entering Wall Drug to sell gold. Now and then you get a bead on the damage to the pole, on the way it's being eaten by sun and rain, gnawed by worms of dawn and dusk, sanded into dust by the wind's steady rub. Better to see the pole from across the street, flushed with the blood-red rays of a melting sun. Seeing the totem close as you pause at the entrance to the Trading Post one April morning, you see your own face forming on the third bird up. And you see the changes again in the women's room mirror. You're only thirty-one, but your face has started to resemble the faces of pioneer women at the Legacy Old Time Photo Shop. There are not many women in the shots of gold rush camps and army stockades, but the ones you've seen have jarred you into feeling like the space between them and you closes, suddenly, on a cold, rainy morning when a thunderclap high above the totem pole fractures the sky.

● ● ●

Hurrying back to work one autumn afternoon after squeezing a haircut and streaking into her lunch hour, Vivian Walsh didn't notice the banks of clouds drifting in from the west or the ashen tint of the skyline toward the freeway or the way that barely visible flakes of snow were flitting from the drooping belly of the sky over town. She saw only the road, which would take her back to Wall Drug for her afternoon shift at Black Hills Gold. Or she saw her own taut, heavily eye-lined face in the rearview mirror as she glanced frequently at her new haircut. She liked what she saw—the sassy, blonde-streaked shortness of her hair—but was feeling twinges of loss, having worn her hair long since high school.

It was simply time, she told herself, you're thirty-one years old, and like Lisa said, the cut took years off your face. Lisa was right; the cut had lifted her cheekbones and made her eyes look larger, more alluring. She had to admit that she hadn't felt this attractive in years. She hoped Cody wouldn't be disappointed. She'd been telling him all summer she was going to do it, just couldn't keep up with the washing and styling. So even though he had a sentimental streak about what her hair did to him the first time he took her on a date, and even though he thought long hair was sexy, he kept telling her it was her hair, do what you want. There had been a little knock in his voice, though. She glanced again at the play of light on the tufts of hair and decided she could always grow it back if she ended up not liking it, or if she sensed Cody cooling toward her physically.

She passed the Dairy Queen and turned on Main, heading toward the business district, which was announced by a series of WALL DRUG AHEAD signs. Glancing at her watch, she realized she had eaten up too much of her lunch hour at the beauty shop, so she eased up over the speed limit, eager to keep her new boss off her neck. It was bad enough hearing sell, sell, sell all the time; she didn't need to be scolded for being late.

As she grew closer to the business district, she noticed for the first time how cold and gray the day had turned from its earlier calm and brightness. The wind was up and was blowing tumbleweeds and whirls of dust across the side streets, and her windshield was starting to dot with flecks of freezing rain that hardened into crystals the wipers couldn't remove.

Vivian didn't slow down to accommodate her reduced vision. She crossed another side street and was about to enter downtown when she had to brake for a STOP sign. Before she could start up again, she heard the drums and trumpets of a high school band, the honking of cars, and the disembodied echo of yelling and cheering voices. Before she could cross the intersection, the Wall High School homecoming parade materialized in all its glorious tawdriness in the intersection.

Vivian's chest muscles tensed, and she was momentarily angry at being prevented from getting back to work on time. Then she re-focused on the ill-fitting uniforms of the marching band, the comical ensemble of short and tall, thick and thin bodies, followed by several recently washed pick-ups and convertibles draped with school-colors streamers, a restored stagecoach pulled by Shetland ponies, and some 4-H horses and riders. And then the homecoming float turned the corner as though birthed from the obscure reaches of the prairie to the west. The float rolled forward into the intersection, Vivian hearing the truck's engine hidden beneath the decks of daisy-yellow facial tissues through her rolled-down window. Her ears keened to the crunch of tires in the street, the rumble and squeak of the makeshift wooden frame that was holding the float together.

For some undetectable reason, the parade halted at that point, as though sensing the dwindling crowds, who were huddled together on the sidewalks or were watching from heated cars or the beds of pick-ups, the watchers bundled against the harsh turn of weather.

It was a beautifully constructed and designed float, far more striking than the one Vivian had ridden on as Homecoming Queen in 1995. But the seating arrangement of the queen's court was similar, and the waving, bare-shouldered queen perched on a stoop of blue and yellow tissues, was a thin, platinum blonde girl with a long neck and an oval face, who looked both lovely and miserable as she hunched beneath the menacing sky. On the lower ledges of the float, her retinue had wrapped themselves in fleece jackets or bright plaid blankets.

Looking up at the girl so isolated and bound to her seat like some tantalizing offering to the gods of deep winter, Vivian suddenly shed her concern about being late for work, or being chewed out, or even being fired. In seconds she was out of her car, removing her new winter jacket as she ran toward the float, hoping the parade would stay stopped for a few more minutes.

As she approached the float, bystanders began yelling catcalls, and a man in a soiled Stetson hollered, "You had your turn, Viv!" Through the laughter and jeers, she circled the float until she saw some wooden steps leading to the top. Then she was on the float, climbing past the astonished faces of the queen's court, jacket in hand, until she was about six feet away from the girl at the top. Up close, the girl was even more attractive and innocent-looking, though her face was blotched red with chill, and her eyes were watering.

"Here," Vivian said, holding the dark pink jacket up. "Take it. You'll catch pneumonia. Why didn't you bring a wrap?"

"I didn't think I'd need one," the girl said.

"Take it and use it," Vivian said firmly, tossing the jacket to her.

Vivian was amused by how deftly and swiftly the girl grabbed the jacket out of the air and how little time she wasted in putting it on. The truck's engine revved suddenly somewhere below them, and the float lurched slightly. Vivian and the girl looked at each other as through a telescopic lens. The girl broke the spell of the moment when she blurted out, "How do I return it?"

"Bring it by the Trading Post tomorrow afternoon. And be sure you keep it on all the way back to the school."

"I will," the girl said, her face beneath the shining prongs of her crown aglow with the blind hopes of youth.

Vivian turned, descended the steps quickly, and hurried back to her car, ignoring the honking and cursing of the drivers backed up behind her at the intersection. Their noise dropped away like the squawks of roosting rooks at the fall of night. The wind had picked up and took swipes at Vivian's bare arms and neck, her unprotected face, but there was very little sting or intimidation to it. The chill could not touch her.

part iii:
ecological angles

I own a South Dakota ranch that has been in the family since my grandfather, a Swedish cobbler, homesteaded here in 1899. Since 1980, I've been active in various environmental affairs, including several statewide battles to contain uranium mining and prevent the establishment of a nuclear waste facility and radioactive waste dump in the state.

● ● ●

Only grass keeps most of the West's thin soil from blowing east in swirling clouds to fall in the Atlantic Ocean. Evolved over millions of years, grasses utilize unique combinations of nutrients and water in specific ways unique to each prairie region. Grass is the main product of Western rangelands. Disturbing the surface of the earth—ploughing and bulldozing space for houses, highways and parking lots—destroys grass and encourages weeds.

. . .The most deliberate way to sell grass—or "realize its market potential" if you think in economic language—is inside a grazing animal.

—Linda Hasselstrom, "Ranching in Western South Dakota"
in *Between Grass and Sky*

When the Buffalo Roam

Henry Bald Eagle Hatches A Dream

Waking from a night of howling wind and collapsing log ashes, Henry Bald Eagle put on a robe and went out into the living room to stoke the fire, the recurring dream he'd had throughout the night turning in bright depictions on the screen of his memory. His wife, Emma, was already up and frying bacon in the kitchen, and he could hear voices on the little television set she'd set on a shelf above her cutting board saying something between surges of static about runaway buffalo. He smiled at the coincidence of the reference, slid another log on the fire, and jostled it into place with a poker. Then he settled back in his rocker to smell the bacon, feel the heat on the soles of his feet, and recount the core of the dream.

When the eagle came close enough to the nest, Henry grabbed its legs, expecting to pull it down into the nest, but instead it bucked hard, its flapping wings thundering in his ears as it lifted up and away from the nest. He had no choice but to hang onto the leathery legs as the eagle carried him out over the plains—the country he'd traveled in a six-passenger airplane in his rodeo days, hitting all the spots on the circuit that looped through Nebraska, eastern Colorado, Oklahoma, Kansas, South Dakota, and North Dakota. In those days the landscape shone in pockets of lights where all the cities and towns scattered across the plains were twinkling with nightlife. By day, there were the glint of car hoods and sheet metal roofs, the glimmer of swimming pools and the green tongues of golf courses, sun flaring off asphalt and the glass faces of office buildings.

In the dream it is summer, the heart of the day, sun burning his face, scorching his lips and ears as he clings to the eagle's legs and soars with it over open land, no cars or roads in sight. No buildings, no glittering roofs, only long stretches of grass, purple mountain spines, winding streams and rivers, and lakes trapped in volcanic bowls. The open land is almost black with the bodies of buffalo, drifting, grazing down the continent, eating their way to the gulf. Sixty million buffalo in a flowing river of horns and wooly necks, dust billowing up around them. Henry's heard about those hunting days, tried to conjure them in his head when the elders told their stories while keeping warm in the terrible winters of '32 and '49. When just a boy he crouched and listened, learning the Lakota world that surged into shape through the tobacco-ruined voices of men with missing teeth and shriveled scrotums and eyes filmed gray with cataracts.

He saw it all now in the dream, reviewed it there in the pocket of his pining fire in a one-story ramshackle house on the Cheyenne River reservation. He flew, glided into the distance of his name, stored the herds of buffalo in the recesses of his brain where the present patterns of Dakota days, of seventy-eight years on this strip of land west of Red Scaffold, remained intact. The imprints of wind and snow, freezing rain, blowing dust, dead cattle, coyote-gutted sheep, eagles drifting in the nothingness of winter noon, frogs frozen deep in the ice-coated edges of Bull Creek. And the senseless stare of the coyote he'd locked eyes with near the empty turkey pen, back in November, way too close for a coyote to come, to let itself be seen, which Henry knew to be a sign of a fierce, bitter winter on the way.

He stored the plane of undulant grass in the folds of his daydream, let go of the eagle's legs when his wife's voice called, "Henry! Time to eat." Her voice cracked the reverie to a hundred shards of light that gathered in the embers of his guttering fire.

● ● ●

The Latter Day Frontiersmen Mobilize
Ernest Bowker, a tire buster at Brunick Brothers Tire and Oil in Clarkston, South Dakota, was there to answer Governor Bill Cosgrove's call for volunteers to help round up a herd of 1,500 runaway buffalo drifting across a twenty-mile stretch of cow country near the Cheyenne River reservation. Standing in the bone-crunching cold of a -49 degree wind-chill factor, Bowker shook his head and snorted when state veterinarian, Stan Morris, told the crowd of snowmobile riders, "They're damn fast. Faster than you can imagine. If some fall down, leave 'em. We'll take care of them later."

"We'll shoot them if we have to," Bowker whispered to his snowmobile partner, Brady Gibson. "Shee-it, man. If you can't ride faster than a buffalo can run, you shouldn't be riding."

Gibson nodded, squinting from the fur-bordered alcove of his parka at the burning white horizon. "Amen," he said. "I'm likin' what he said about shootin', too, if we have to."

"He stole that idea from Governor Cosgrove, the bastard. What's with these Fish and Game guys anyway?"

"He's a vet, not a ranger, dingbat. But he's still small potatoes, like you say."

"We're wasting time worryin' about it," Bowker said. "Let's ride. We got buffalo to save."

● ● ●

A Cub Reporter Interviews the Owner of the Triple Q Ranch
That same afternoon, Kate Stewart—owner of the Triple Q Ranch—told reporter Terrence Moody for the third time in their fifteen-minute conversation at the Cheyenne River Café, "We don't have brucellosis. There've been no reported cases of it in South Dakota since 1990."

"Is it true that the only way for a cow to get brucellosis is by licking or eating the aborted fetus of a buffalo?"

"That's the most common way. Sometimes from eating hay that buffalo have urinated on. Fifteen hundred were loose. Members of my family, plus the ranch crew and several neighbors, have already rounded up about twelve hundred, brought them back with helicopters."

"How did they get loose to start with?"

"The wind blew drifts along the fence line until the top wires were covered, and then the temperature dropped and the drifts iced over. The buffalo just waked across the drifts and kept going."

"But if the fence line is still covered with snow, I don't see how you'll be able to keep the twelve hundred you've got from getting out again."

"We're plowing the drifts away from the fence line."

"I see. Well then, what are the chances you'll get the other three hundred buffalo back?"

"In this weather, not good."

"So if they have that disease, they'll spread it all over once the cows start licking the carcasses in the spring."

"If they died, there wouldn't be anything left to lick. Coyotes and buzzards would pick the bones clean. But they won't die. This is their kind of weather. They'll just move with it until they find food and shelter."

"This is the worst winter storm in years, though. Maybe the worst ever."

"No one's told the buffalo that. Now if you'll excuse me, Mr. Moody, I need to get back to the ranch. I have a long night ahead of me."

"It's been a pleasure, Ms. Stewart. As for this crisis, you can count me to tell it like it is. Oh, and the coffee is on me."

"I'll never forget you, Mr. Moody."

● ● ●

The LDFS Loses a Member

Ernest Bowker swerved to the left and Brady Gibson to the right, both men determined to force this last buffalo bull into reversing its direction and to steer it back toward the rest of the herd. It was a massive bull with a long, ice-covered beard and thick black wool around its neck and head. Even in snow to its hips, it looked like a battleship plowing the sea. Its head was lowered slightly, horn tips flashing in the dying sun while the broad shoulders knocked banks of snow out of its path.

Ernest and Brady had to pour on the gas to close on the buffalo, yelling and yipping to let it know that escape was futile.

"He's ignoring us," Bowker yelled above the wind and the chuffing, snorting buffalo. "I'll swing out and cut him off, force him to turn."

"Don't get too close," Gibson yelled, but just then Bowker cut in front of the buffalo, raising a wide spray of snow as he leaned to keep from tipping the snowmobile over. He shot out ahead of the buffalo; then, to Gibson's amazement and horror, hit the brake and swung the snowmobile around to face the buffalo.

The snowmobile's engine died the same instant Bowker realized that the buffalo was not going to stop or turn but had picked up speed and was charging across a low spot of ground the wind had scooped out.

What happened next Brady Gibson would be talking about in bars and cafes in a widening circle throughout central South Dakota for the next ten years. He would repeat it at every campout and mock buffalo hunt for the Latter Day Frontiersman Society on the banks of the Missouri River summer nights when the wind was low in the buffalo grass and the cup of the Big Dipper was tilted toward the Black Hills. He would tell it with a mixture of guilt, awe, terror, and disbelief, polishing the details to rub the dreamlike luster off it and make it real, make it right, in homage to Ernest Bowker.

During the fifteen seconds it took the buffalo to reach Bowker's snowmobile, the wind seemed to drop, the air stood still, the sky locked into a sickening, cider-colored light, and Gibson could hear Bowker shouting, "Shoot, Brady! For God's sake, shoot!"

Gibson had time to shout only once, "I can't pull the trigger, I can't pull the trigger! My fingers is froze!" before the buffalo's head collided with the snowmobile's windshield, flattening it into Bowker's lap and flipping him up in the air, kicking, doll-like, before he landed on the buffalo's horns. The buffalo jerked its head and flung Bowker back up in the air and into a drift, which soon darkened with the stains of his blood.

The buffalo steadied itself in a new determination to follow the wind, paused, and turned to glance at Gibson sitting paralyzed on the other snowmobile. Then it waded into the darkening shadows of some nearby pines.

Gibson did not give chase.

● ● ●

The Rancher Paints a Still Life

Kate Stewart was sorry to hear about the death of Ernest Bowker. She was sorry to hear about the injuries and frostbite suffered by eleven other roundup volunteers. She was sorry about the sixteen buffalo that had to be shot and the thirty-seven others that were still missing. But as she floated in a small aircraft above the rolling hills and flatlands of the Triple Q Ranch, looked with rapt attention across snow-covered crests and draws, and saw the expanding, contracting clusters of buffalo dotting the winter landscape, she was glad to have this portion of the herd back. She was glad to see their indolent drift in the wind, their stationary patches on the prairie's white face. And she rejoiced in this private tableau of dark, distant figures fused in a time-erasing privacy with snow.

Crop Duster

EVEN THOUGH ROLAND IVERSON HAD grown tired of living in Vermillion, South Dakota, a place he'd grown up in, he never grew tired of flying his crop dusting airplane, which he was going to be doing in about fifteen minutes. This first flight of the season would carry him over the farm fields surrounding the town and over the winding, serpentine shape of the Vermillion River and the little prairie towns sprinkled across the two counties his crop dusting contracts covered. Sitting in the cockpit, making all his last minute preparations, he could feel the excitement mounting. Something about seeing it all from the sky, the way an eagle might, restored its pastoral innocence and made everything look far more clean and orderly than it actually was.

At one time Roland had been able to reverse the bird's-eye perspective by peering from the ground at objects in the sky, night or day. This was back in the 1970s when the University of South Dakota had a state-of-the-art telescope mounted on the roof of the central administration building. Dr. Calvin Adams, from whom Roland had taken an astronomy course in the mid-1970s, had taken him up to the roof on several occasions and taught him the intricacies of using the telescope. The boundless blackness of the night sky and the scattering of stars and planets across a void too deep to comprehend had dwarfed the town and shrunk its virtues and skullduggery to a grain of sand. Once the telescope was taken off the roof of Slagle Hall and the other observatory on the north side of campus was dismantled and junked, he lost his ground-to-sky window, and by the arrival of the 1990s he had to rely solely on the early spring crop dusting outlook for the balance he needed.

And he needed the balance often. He had lived in Clay County most of his life, gone to high school at Vermillion High, built houses for twenty-five years before becoming disillusioned with the building industry and starting his crop spraying business, served on the city council, the arts council, and the fair board, and knew a great deal about the town's virtues and accomplishments, and a good portion of its dirt. More, really, than he wanted to know. He knew who the slumlords were and the way they endangered the lives of the students they rented to with their dilapidated, roach-infested firetraps; knew who was bedding whose wife and who was screwing the taxpayers on the new golf course development east of town. He'd seen the down-and-dirty maneuvers of small town shakers and movers, heard about the things they did, the tricks they used to get their way, the moves they made to keep their sons and daughters out of jail. He knew what went on in the city council chambers—the meetings before the meetings— knew about the bookie joints in the back rooms of local bars, the bribing of cops and sheriff's deputies.

Roland had come to see it all as relative, as no worse than what went on in other small towns scattered along the I-29 corridor. He'd heard about the drug-dealing owner of the Greenfield Dairy Queen, a thirty-six-year-old "family man" famous for seducing and impregnating his high school counter girls. He felt that this was no different than what was happening in the larger towns—Sioux Falls to the north and Sioux City, Iowa, to the south. So even without the secret support of the Slagle Hall telescope and the nihilistic fantasies it offered him, he could still keep the town and its dark doings in perspective from the distance of the afternoon sky, from an angle that allowed only rooftops, treetops, and tranquil streets to be seen by the naked eye.

The separation, the movement through a different band of light, also helped him keep in mind the good side of Vermillion, helped him see the determination in the decent folks he knew, in the clubs and organizations that kept the whole place moving in good directions, kept the town's appearance up, tended to the elderly, and watched out for kids. He had known large numbers of generous, kind-hearted people, hard workers, selfless volunteers, loyal to every cause and event that went on. There was no shortage of them in the town; it was just that they got over-shadowed, as at the national level, by the blackguards and crooks.

He sometimes thought of the pluses and minuses the way he thought of this river-bottom town's wild life—a quirky confluence of tanagers, monarch butterflies, and fleet-footed deer with all manner of rodents and snakes, spiders and slimy-lipped carp, and all the raging insects who gathered in the weeds and on the stagnant ponds. They all played a part in the make-up of a place he'd come to see as a blessing and a curse, a place you had to get some distance on to understand. That was what made the first airplane flights of spring uplifting and unique—a shift in how he saw the motley town. And it also served as a reminder that he could leave and go to a different place when the time came to do so. The trick was to finish his career out and still have some hope, still believe the world had a fighting chance. Sometimes the signs seemed faint, and you had to look hard to see hope. From the sky, he could look again.

Rising off the tarmac at the Vermillion airport, Roland felt the old thrill of being airborne, the sudden openness of a boundless sky, and could feel the burden and disenchantment of being cooped up all winter peeling off him and falling away.

He flew the plane cautiously but smoothly, regaining his familiarity with the instrument panel and feeling more young and bold and robust as he climbed farther and farther above the patchwork design of corn stubble fields, greening meadows, and black dirt feedlots. The land flared out under him with a glorious sense of rebirth and promise, and he was back in a good place in his mind.

He could see that a long stretch of the Missouri River west of town had shifted to the south over the winter, covering some of the land he'd dusted last year and seeping away from the mud-covered path it had been following. Once again he was reminded of how much had changed in both the town and out on the prairie just in the years he'd been dusting, and he suddenly found himself remembering a different time and place.

Looking at the smooth, open sweep of fields dotted with the stubs of last fall's cornstalks, he was remembering how, as a student at Vermillion High School, he had taken a shotgun to school so that he could hunt gophers or rabbits while walking home from school to his house on the edge of town. He had kept the shotgun in his locker, the way some kids kept baseball gloves or football shoes, and no one thought anything of it. He could imagine what would happen to any kid who brought a shotgun to school these days. The kid would be on the floor in handcuffs, and the school would be empty in fifteen minutes.

A damn shame to have things get so paranoid and crazy, but turn on the TV or pick up a newspaper and it was easy to appreciate the worry and fear you could feel in the air. "Read the paper," is what he would say to Karla every time they argued about the condition of the world. He had said it to her three or four times last night over dinner on the patio.

"It's the same country it's always been," Karla said halfway through the meal.

"Can't see it," Roland said. "It's not the America I grew up in. All these damn drugs and guns, and the way people talk to each other on the television shows. Just plain rude and crude. Can you imagine what it's like to teach high school now?"

"You're overreacting," Karla said. "There's just more honesty now, more information. Mass media has simply unfastened the Victorian chastity belt and thrown it away."

"Whose chastity belt?"

"Just a metaphor. What I meant was that things like the Internet are only making public what was there all along, clear back to the Depression if you want to talk about drugs and guns. You think we'd have the same opinion of George Washington if we knew about him what we know about JFK?"

Roland had set down the rib bone he'd been gnawing on, taken a long drink of beer, and said, "You've been at the University too long, Karla. Things just aren't the same as they used to be. I swear they aren't. There's something different; something mean and nasty in the way we live now."

"Old as the hills," Karla said. "Want some lemon pie?"

Thinking now about the slice of chilled lemon pie seemed to soothe his spirit. He sensed Karla could be right; there were plenty of people he talked to at the Hangar Bar who agreed with her. Still, he couldn't concede to the idea that the world was in decent shape, considering what he was seeing and hearing day to day. There was more to it than some new honesty.

Out here in the blue expanse of a South Dakota sky, he could lose his pessimism and irritation with the condition of so-called civilization and feel a surge of renewal, of the old beauty, the timeless play of color and light. He could see from the changes in the land and the grid of roads that he was approaching Ted Heine's property, so he started his preparation for dusting an extensive swath of fields to the east, then curving north and catching three other farms along the Missouri

River before heading into Union County for the final pass of the afternoon over the Carlson place.

He set the dials for the tanks and activated the lines, gradually lowering the plane toward a line of trees to his right. The plane jerked and the engine sputtered a little, reminding him that this business had a dangerous side to it. Several situations in which he'd come close to crashing flashed through his mind.

He had to keep an eye out at all times for power lines and silos and radio station transmitters, the new wind energy turbines, and even birds, especially the eagles that nested and hunted along the shores of the Missouri. They were an inspiring sight—even more stunning when seen riding the air currents from another point in the sky than from the ground, and the way they changed color as they dipped and turned in the sun. They were one of the variables of a job he'd grown too familiar with, and he was always glad for the break in routine their magic shows gave him.

Their presence reminded him, too, of the changes that had come with the environmental movement and how there were now people in town protesting crop spraying and mosquito spraying, and every other kind of spraying, and the use of pesticides by farmers. And there were the Missouri River activists at the University with their criticisms of the Army Corps of Engineers and their protests about all the dams on the Missouri River, and what the dams were doing to wildlife and what crop spraying was doing to drinking water.

Whenever he thought about all the complications and strife, he was glad he wouldn't be in the crop dusting business much longer. Once his wife retired from teaching, he'd quit spraying, and they'd move to Colorado. He'd read an article in the paper just last week about crop dusting planes being vandalized in Minnesota by an eco-militant group that had also claimed credit for setting fire to some buildings at a turkey processing plant. He couldn't understand such thinking. It was like Bin Laden and his gang of holy hoodlums. That kind of destructiveness accomplished nothing.

Roland swung the plane out into the drop position and opened the tanks, watching the cloud of crop dust billow out below him. He guided its shape and movement like a big city baker spreading frosting on an expensive wedding cake, then looped around and swept down over the fields on the west side of the property, the drone of the engine buzzing steadily through the radiant blue air. He felt the old harmony of flight over open land, the pleasure of doing work with precision, restricting the crop treatment to very specific sections of land and dodging the areas he was expected to avoid. He took pride in keeping the spray where it belonged even if that meant taking some risks with the airplane. He sometimes wished he could take in the cockpit with him some of the people who presumed that crop dusting was reckless and haphazard and subject to the vagaries of the wind. There were times when the wind sabotaged his efforts, but for the most part he rarely missed the target.

Things were going that way today, and Roland was so pleased by the drops he was making that he eased off his guard, crossed into Union County, and flew down over some unfamiliar fields. Before he could get his bearings, a white pick-up truck, which had just emerged from a dense windbreak of trees, swerved out into the field and stopped. A man in black pants, a dark shirt, and a baseball cap jumped out of the pick-up with a rifle in his hands and began shaking his fist at Roland's plane. Then he went down on one knee, took aim, and started firing.

Before Roland could lift the nose of the plane up and swing out of range, bullets were zipping past the windshield and ricocheting off the fuselage, one of them clipping a small piece off the edge of the left wing.

"Crazy bastard!" Roland hollered as he gunned the engine in a mad hurry to get out of the rifle's range. He roared up toward a cloud bank and arced to his right, climbing quickly and escaping any more bullets.

He was so shaken he almost landed the plane in one of Earl Merrigan's fields, but decided to do the dusting Earl had asked him to do. By the time he finished this last job, he had only enough gas to get back to the Vermillion airport and coast into the hangar.

* * *

Once he parked the plane and turned off the engine, Roland sat there staring at the landing strip, at the silver-green fields of weeds beyond the strip, and the hazy blue bluffs above the Missouri River. He was glad to be back on the ground, and he was thinking more than ever that this would be his last year to fly. He would tell his friends at the Hangar Bar about being shot at, but he wouldn't tell Karla because she'd want him out of the sky immediately. But you couldn't let one misguided crackpot scare you off. He thought maybe he should drive over to Union County and find out who that bastard was, drag him out of his pick-up, and beat the tar out of him, but, on second thought, decided to leave well enough alone. No telling what something like that might turn into.

He climbed out of the plane and was hanging his helmet and flight clothing in a locker when he heard some racket in the rear of the hangar. At first he thought it was a cat after a mouse or maybe scrapping with another cat. So he walked around his plane and pulled the string on a light over a workbench.

He couldn't see anything at first; then he saw the black body and the white stripes. The skunk was hunkered in the corner with its back to Roland, but when Roland stepped closer, the skunk whirled around and charged past him, and he saw that its head was stuck in a plastic peanut butter jar, which rattled and clattered as the skunk skittered under the plane and out the other side, running into the empty hangar next door and bumping into posts, boxes, and metal locker doors. It clawed repeatedly at the rim of the jar, but couldn't pull the jar off its head. The skunk's frenzy and confusion were both comical and pathetic.

For a moment Roland was tempted to go get in his car and head down the road to the Hangar Bar. He needed a drink, and he needed to tell someone about being shot at. The skunk would just have to fight its way out of the jar. But he could see from the way the skunk's head was starting to swell that it was going to become impossible for the skunk to free itself of the jar.

For the next half hour, Roland chased the skunk around the hangar until he was finally able to pin its tail down with an airplane windshield squeegee, press the bobbing tip to the floor with his boot, and hold it there. Then he very slowly split the jar down the side with a pair of tin snips until the skunk's head was suddenly poking out. The jar was still hanging by a strand of plastic around the skunk's neck but looked like it would come off if the skunk made the right moves.

Roland kept his foot on the tail as he eased the squeegee off the skunk's torso, then he turned everything loose and backed up as fast as he could. The skunk leaped to its feet and darted away without raising its tail, much to Roland's relief. He watched the skunk scurry across the runway, dragging the flopping jar. The jar came off just before the skunk disappeared in the field beyond the runway.

● ● ●

Roland felt uplifted, exhilarated at seeing the skunk enter the field, but a residue of anger at being shot at a few hours earlier was still stirring in him. So instead of turning left at the junction, he turned east in the direction of Union County, heading, on a hunch, for the Wagon Wheel Inn on the outskirts of the tiny town of Spink. He wasn't sure what he was going to do if he spotted the white pick-up in the Wagon Wheel parking lot; he just knew he had to drive there. He hadn't been in a bar fight in at least twenty years, but he could feel the tension in his blood flowing into his fists.

He pulled into the Wagon Wheel parking lot and drove between two rows of cars and trucks whose windshields flared and flickered in the late afternoon sun. He slowed to a crawl, hoping to spot the the truck as he remembered it—a fairly late model with extra tires, gas cans, and tools in the bed. There were no pick-ups in the open lot, but to his irritation and confusion there were three white pick-ups nosed up to the front of the stucco building, all of them newer models with tires, gas cans, and tools in the bed. He knew then that it would be impossible to identify the driver he was after without calling out the whole bar.

He eased into a shaded spot under a billboard west of the building and turned his engine off. He could still feel the urge down in his diaphragm to bloody someone's nose. But as his engine began its intermittent clicking as it cooled, a sense of distortion and futility took hold of him. And even though there was a fair chance he was only fifty feet from the shooter, a cold logic replaced his hostility with a sudden distance on the whole incident. What had happened over that field was not really that outrageous or surprising. The shooter's reaction was an extreme viewpoint that fit the times. Just a different world now, and further evidence of the troubling cross-currents he was only too keenly aware of. So why respond in kind? He started his engine and drove away quickly.

● ● ●

By the time Roland sat down at his usual spot at the Hangar Bar and looked at two of his oldest friends sitting there grinning at him like a pair of gray-whiskered Labradors, he was ready to tell them about the whole afternoon. He would start with the skunk incident and work backwards. There were already two schooners of beer lined up in front of him.

To his surprise, he had so much fun telling the skunk story and then another story about a one-eyed Jack Russell dog he used to take crop dusting with him, and another story about the first time he noodled a catfish, that he felt no need to disclose the shooting incident and spoil the mood; maybe tell it another time.

Standing there in the neon-reddened light, smelling beer and broasted chicken grease, the jukebox pounding and people's strident, laughing voices flitting around the room like a flock of jabbering birds concealed in the creeping blue smoke, he felt as though his arms had lengthened exponentially, as though he could hold the world, with all its grit and sinew, at bay.

Deer on the Runway

"JOHN MADDEN IS RIGHT," DEREK Hesla said to his wife, Beverly, who was taking a catnap in the aisle seat next to him.

Beverly's eyes flipped open, and without looking at him, she said, "Who's John Madden?"

"NFL broadcaster," Hesla said. "Rides a bus all over the US to cover Monday Night Football games because he won't fly."

"You mean he's never flown?"

"He's flown; he just quit. Paranoia got him, long before 9/11."

"He must be really spooked."

"Actually, he probably just got bored with this whole scene. How long have we been sitting here?"

"About forty-five minutes."

"Seems longer."

Hesla leaned forward to look at the rows of heads encapsulated by what he thought of as the fiberglass sarcophagus of the airplane, with its reading lights and warning lights and long, tubular luggage compartments, its sardine-stuffed rows of seats with their cookie cutter headrests, and its EXIT doors. Toward the front of the cabin, flight attendants flitted around, ducking behind the ever-mysterious First Class curtains and the steel-barred cockpit door, and then reappearing with blankets and pillows and meandering down the center aisle to distribute them to passengers in coach. One of the attendants had come on the intercom two or three times already to apologize for the delayed departure, her explanation involving late cargo and something about landing gear. Now she came on the speaker again to direct that all food trays be stored, all cell phones shut off, and all seat belts fastened for takeoff.

At the attendant's commands, the Puget Sound security company executive sitting behind the Heslas paused to clear his throat, then continued the elaborate narrative he'd been spooling out while they'd been sitting on the tarmac to a sometime business associate he'd inadvertently run into upon boarding the plane. Their seats happened to be right across the aisle from each other farther back in the tail of the aircraft than even the Heslas were sitting. The security company executive, who had groused lightly while making his way down the aisle about being sent to the rear of the class, seemed to have forgotten his placement on the plane quickly when presented with the chance to talk about his employer to the eager-to-listen acquaintance, who, in the few sentences he was able to interject at the start of the conversation, explained that he was "on the market" even though he had a decent position with the company he was working for as a sales rep.

So the security company executive spared him no information in telling him all the company had done since 9/11 to protect the Washington coastline and the plans the company had to work with the US Coast Guard and all the international shipping companies, and how much money the company had spent to protect the ferryboat industry, and how many promotions he'd had and how many times he'd been on the phone with Homeland Security, and how proud he was of the company's rallying to join the war on terror. And all of the different ways the company was diversifying and what problems the company was having with its stockholders and with large container imports, and how long it was going to take the company to develop a new computer system that would revolutionize coastline security, thanks to the company's board of directors and the relationship between the company and the Seattle business community, especially Microsoft. He just hoped that the company would be able to get the support it deserved from the federal government and the Puget Sound Port Authority. The company was willing to go the extra mile because the company put national security first. He couldn't believe how lucky he was to be working for a company of that caliber.

"Are we there yet?" he said suddenly, only a few seconds after the pilot's announcement of takeoff.

The man listening to the executive responded with a patronizing laugh. Hesla looked at Beverly, then leaned toward her and said in a low voice, "Are we going to have to listen to this all the way to Seattle?"

"Afraid so," she said. "He hasn't gotten to family yet."

Hesla rolled his eyes. "Got any Dramamine?"

Beverly grinned.

"Sorry. I suppose you could drink three or four bourbons."

"That would only get me in a perverse mood," he said. "No telling what I might say or do."

"Maybe he'll ease off and take a nap once we get up in the air."

"Fat chance," Hesla said. "Windbags don't nap. Too much air pressure."

"Think about our new grandson," Beverly said. "Close him out."

Just then the lights dimmed in the cabin, and they could feel the plane gaining speed as it made its taxi maneuvers down the runway and began to rev its engines.

Takeoff was the one part of flying Hesla disliked the most. It always made his stomach drop and his hands grip the armrests, and it flipped his mind out into an anticipation of a sudden loss of power and a careening spiral to the ground. And there was something about seeing a section of city—the tin roofs, the smoke of industrial parks, the highways crawling with cars—that added to the foreboding, which suggested no way out. The only distraction he'd ever been able to find some counterpoint in was to look out the window at whatever natural scenery might be in view.

Hesla adjusted his seatbelt, leaned closer to the window, and fixed his eyes on the sun-struck fields beyond the fence as the plane picked up speed. The increasing volume of the engine muted the drone of the security company executive, who was now detailing his daughter's plans for medical school. Or maybe law school. She'd killed both the MCAT and the LSAT. Couldn't decide what she really wanted, there were so many schools wanting her. Plus, a bunch of suitors were clouding the picture now that she had her own apartment. Hot and cold running guys. Overall, she favored U of Chicago, was weighing out Johns Hopkins and Georgetown. She had no plans to get serious with any of the boyfriends, not with the things she had her sights set on.

Hesla waited for the sudden lift that signaled takeoff, his eyes glued to the thicket of bramble and pine trees being chiseled from the early morning fog by a rising sun. Just when the plane had reached the furious ground speed necessary to lift it off the ground, two deer bolted from a field adjacent to the runway, heading straight for the fence: a large, graceful, older buck with a stunning rack and a young buck with spike antlers. Hesla panicked for a second, then eased back into a confidence that the fence was far too high for the deer to leap. He'd never seen a cyclone fence that high. To his shock and amazement a few seconds later, the larger buck surged down the slope and cleared the fence in what seemed a miraculous leap, followed by the younger deer, which also easily cleared the fence. Then both darted straight across the runway and were lost from sight. When the plane suddenly lurched like it was bouncing over a rut, and a distant but very real thud sounded just as they lifted off the tarmac, Hesla knew they had hit one or both deer.

"Damn!"

"What?" Beverly said. "What's wrong?"

"Did we hit something?" the security executive said to one of the attendants near the rear of the plane.

"I'm not sure," she said.

The plane continued forward, the control tower coming into view as they rose several hundred feet then began a slow loop back toward the runway.

The pilot's voice had the usual unruffled tone as he explained that they'd hit a deer and were going to have to return to the ground. Hesla winced at the thought of a deer being clobbered by the fuselage or beheaded by a wing, its head flipping up into one of the engines.

"Same-O, same-O," the security executive said. "If it's not one thing, it's another. They damn well better get me to Seattle on time. I'm a day behind already."

Hesla had to fight off the urge to jump up and call the man an asshole or whatever else came to mind. Beverly put her hand on his forearm and said, "If we're lucky, they'll put him on a different plane."

"I knew there was a reason I traveled with you," Hesla said, his spirits lifted by the prospect of a quiet, private flight.

"Actually I was fantasizing that he'd choke on a pretzel and have to stop talking."

Hesla nodded, then glanced back out the window as the plane's landing gear thumped down hard, and they began a slow taxi toward the terminal. The cyclone fence and the patch of trees the deer had run out of came back into view. Looking at the height of the fence, Hesla was still amazed that the deer had cleared it. That was what he loved about wildlife and why he'd spent so many years with the South Dakota Department of Game, Fish, and Parks. Animals and birds always had one more move you couldn't predict; not that instincts defied explanation. Their innate powers were struggling to keep things even with the way humans were encroaching on their habitats, driving them into harm's way.

Back home in South Dakota, the Sioux Falls airport had been doing all kinds of things to keep Canada geese off the runway when they dropped into the marshes near the airport on their way south in October. Danger to humans made whatever action the city decided to take an automatically indisputable choice: the geese could not be tolerated. The city's resolve made sense to an extent, except that it fed an increasing intolerance he saw in society's attitude toward anything that got in the way of its growth and pleasures, its appetite for more of everything.

All around Hesla and his wife passengers were standing, shuffling coats and bags, opening luggage compartments as a buzz of conversation ran up and down the brightly lit cabin. Hesla could hear bits and pieces of comments about the deer: "I think just one . . ." "No way he could stop at that point."

The security executive chimed in with, "Well, it's too bad, but it's bound to happen with deer, just like on the freeway. We're lucky we didn't crash."

"That's for sure," his companion sided, "Better him than us. Oh, by the way, here's my card in case you hear of any openings."

Hesla stood and followed Beverly into the aisle, eager to board the other plane and get on with the trip.

● ● ●

As it turned out, they were given seats toward the front of another plane and saw no more of the Puget Sound security executive. They had a smooth trip to Seattle and spent the Thanksgiving weekend in good company. Their new grandson awakened a fresh sense of time and future in them, made them feel grateful to be alive. The weather in Puget Sound was such that they were able to do some hiking and beach combing, and to visit the Seattle Zoo and the Seattle Aquarium.

At the aquarium Hesla felt strongly drawn to the tanks of intricate sea life—the urchins and sponges, the stingrays and squids—and felt an uplifting fascination with the boundless waters of the world when he glanced out the plate glass windows on the wharf side of the sound. But what stuck with him most was the taxidermy figure of a great white shark he discovered when he drifted off to the other side of the aquarium on his own and happened to look up. He hadn't realized he was standing under the shark, which was suspended by steel cables attached to the ceiling, and it was like a leap through time to be poised incongruously fifteen feet beneath a creature whose shocking size and ferocious bearing seemed to squelch his protective connection with civilization.

He had never been in close proximity to a shark of any kind, and even though his logic reassured him that the Great White was frozen in the stillness of death, the long, Learjet belly and the ghastly rows of teeth struck an unorthodox awe in his heart. The awe was amplified when he read on the exhibit poster fastened to a support beam the story of the shark's capture. The poster told how, in the late 1970s, the shark had gotten tangled in some fishing nets not far from shore and was killed and hauled in by a group of fishing boats. But the part of the story that stood out most to Hesla and reinforced the blood-chilling bulk of the shark's twenty-foot, four-thousand-pound body were the sentences about the fishermen finding, upon opening the shark's belly, two adult sea lions, their bodies fully intact. The shark had swallowed them whole.

When Hesla looked again at the shark suspended in the jaundiced gray light of a Seattle morning, his trip to the coast jumped to the level of ancient dream. The image of the shark floating in the eerie white sky of the aquarium was seared into his memory, and the humbling power of the imprint triggered a swift recollection of the sultry June afternoon in a South Dakota cornfield when he'd nearly been struck by lightning. Knocked to the ground by the strike, he'd felt, upon waking up, a tingling, telescopic distance on the puniness of the human enterprise—a perspective he'd stored like bullion in a sealed part of his mind. The shark's dauntless, godlike aura triggered a similar distancing of his mind and spirit.

Even after they left the aquarium and headed to Pike's Place Market for lunch, it was not easy for Hesla to re-connect with family and city. It was not until a day or two later that he began to appreciate the environmental spirit of his daughter and son-in-law and the things he and Beverly saw and heard once they immersed themselves in the raven and totem pole culture of the Pacific Northwest. It was clear the population revered the beauty of the mountains, woods, and waterways and had taken steps to live in harmony with such a beautiful ecosystem. It was easy to see how one could be inspired to do so.

The jutting mountain skyline, the lighting, the lush, abundant greenery, and the subtlety of ocean breezes had a purging effect on both Hesla and Beverly, and they flew back over the continental divide into Denver uplifted and refreshed by what they'd heard and seen. Yet there had been a heckling echo of wariness haunting Hesla's reflections on the amount of traffic, people, cement, and asphalt he'd seen, and on all the houses perched on every slope and promontory. Civilization was clearly exploding on that coastline and putting major stress on the entire Puget Sound. Could the impassioned environmentalists actually keep the balance they claimed came first? The question nagged and needled him at the SeaTac airport terminal and on both legs of the flight back home.

Just before they landed in Omaha, Hesla turned his thinking to a more positive side and said a prayer of thanks for the birth of his grandson, who had looked at him with the nonchalance of someone in possession of boundless hope and energy. The child's eyes seemed to contain an agenda the earth itself was harboring in spite of our flagrant disregard for it. He did not think of the look as a spiritual thing but as a life thing, but he decided by the time they landed that maybe it actually was spiritual in nature.

● ● ●

On the Sunday morning following their return to South Dakota, Hesla skipped church and drove out to Randy Mollet's farm to check for beavers. He'd helped Randy introduce them to the stream on the east edge of the property in hopes of gaining the best possible natural balance of land and wildlife. With what beavers know about caring for water, beavers were the key to the optimal well-being of all the other species.

Hesla drove to his favorite section of the farm, just off Highway 50 east of Vermillion, and walked away from the highway toward the dirt road that curved around the tilting gravestones of a pioneer cemetery and was swallowed by a dip into a ravine where the stream ran. In its stubble-dotted flatness and its dark dirt and in the stark beauty of its separation from the town and highway, the field was like a throw-back to prehistoric times. There was a tranquility he'd felt only here, on this five-acre section of sun-dried dirt, less than five miles from the I-29 corridor.

The stream wound along the field's edge and was swallowed by buck brush and brambles as the land rippled away in gold and charcoal wrinkles that merged with distant bands of haze. Walking along in the frost-coated grass that sloped toward the stream, he could feel, even though he couldn't see them, the furred and feathered denizens of this place: deer, rabbits, foxes, hawks, raccoons, muskrats, and wild turkeys. They dwelled here in a privacy that pre-dated South Dakota, the United States, the Plains Indians, and every other human group to ever walk or ride across the land's ever-changing surface.

He could see the beaten-down paths, the corn stubble that deer had sucked and licked the molasses out of during the full-moon night when their vision was keenest, when the world of dirt-clod and tree line was theirs. They'd been out here taking their due from the stalks and nibbling the yellowing leaves of young ash trees. With them, raccoons roamed the cornrows, opossums trotted along the field's shadowed edge, foxes crawled from their dens, red fur glowing in the moon-soaked air. The night was their time and they used it superbly, vanishing by dawn as though no living creature were to be found here.

So he was surprised to see two young deer—a buck and a doe—down at the lower end of the field closest to the thicket, still out in the growing light of day, nibbling on corn stalks. Hesla dropped down a bank, the deer slipping from sight as he moved along the stream looking for beaver signs. Now and then he moved up the slope, peering through the network of branches at the grazing deer. At first he didn't realize the buck was closing in on the doe, eyeing her steadily whenever she dropped her head to suck on a stalk. Hesla guessed that she'd passed the tree where the buck had rubbed the velvet off his antlers and then scented the grass at the base of the tree with his urine. In obedience to the dictates of her body, the doe had added her own urine to the patch of grass—a message the buck had read this morning before lifting his freshly antlered head to see the doe standing in the field.

The buck wove a tightening circle, meandering toward the doe, and Hesla was struck by the patience with which the buck moved toward mating. The doe was clearly too young, too inexperienced to know what she was supposed to do, and in her skittish awkwardness, appeared to be on the verge of bolting into the trees. The buck waited. He was patient in the extreme. He was the last gentleman in America. In the barely audible whisper of leaves he waited, accommodating the doe's hesitation.

The doe continued to lean and nibble and glance and wait and turn and pause. Before long, the buck had come closer and closer, eyes fixed on her every move. Standing beside her, facing the other direction, he brushed against her hip, trotted forward, then pivoted and tried to mount her. She wiggled away and ran a few yards as though frightened or confused. The buck stood watching her back legs and rump. Then he came forward again and leaned toward her tail to sniff the air, confirming what he already knew as he tossed his head back and closed on her again, front hooves locking into place on her flanks.

Hesla watched the frenzied breeding only a few seconds, decided he'd seen more than he had any right to see, turned back toward the stream, feeling a humbling sense of gratitude. Half an hour later he spotted several sapling trunks chewed like half-sharpened lead pencils, then saw a beaver slip out of a stand of reeds and darken the stream with its fluid mahogany shape. Farther on, he saw the intricate weave of driftwood and peeled branches that signaled the beginnings of a dam. It was a moment equal to or greater than anything he'd seen in the Pacific Northwest, and it made him wish things could stay like this forever.

He took hope for this idea from the fact that the environmental organizations he had supported and participated in the past ten years had actually stopped the construction of a large refinery a Texas oil company was trying to build at Elk Point, just fifteen miles southeast of where he was standing. The odds had been heavily against such hopes, especially back in 2006 when dozens of Union County farmers had signed confidentiality agreements to sell their land to Hyperion. The whole secretive scheme, labeled The Gorilla Project by wary locals because of some stone gorillas near a statuary fence line in Union County, had pitted brother against brother and neighbor against neighbor. The strife and anxiety were glaring at all the meetings Hesla attended once the state of South Dakota granted Hyperion an air quality permit in 2008. But he had still been heartened by the passion and courage of the people he met and worked with in Save Union County, Citizens Opposed to Oil Pollution, and the Sierra Club. The size of the project—a $10 billion refinery on 3300 acres of land, using twelve million gallons of Big Sioux and Missouri River water a day to process four hundred thousand barrels of Canadian tar sands oil—was terrifying to Hesla. But the energy and faith of the resistance groups had made a believer of him.

Even when Union County residents voted in favor of the refinery in 2008, he didn't lose hope. Or when Hyperion announced a construction target date of 2011. And when the tide turned that same year with Hyperion halting construction due to the national recession, and with the simultaneous legal delay of the Keystone XL Pipeline project that was threatening the Ogallala Aquifer in Nebraska, he was elated. As soon as

Hyperion began letting their land lease options expire in 2012 and did not follow through in 2013 on their one-year extension for lease renewals, Hesla knew the refinery was dead.

He smiled and shook his head at the outcome of it all and then turned and climbed the bank so that he was again on eye level with the empty field. It shone with a tragic radiance in the wash of November light. Echoing in his head were the redundant pronouncements of voices he'd heard so many times in the everyday drift of his life, saying, "You can't stand in the way of progress."

Turning toward the withered stalks along the field's east edge, he stared at the spot where the deer had been mating. In spite of all desires to the contrary, he had to concede that it was difficult to stand in the way of progress, or, as he preferred to think of it, the relentless advancement of change. Still, there were times that, if you were determined and vigilant, you could stand in the way of progress, as the local resistance to Hyperion had proven. Or, on another level, you could stand outside of progress as he was doing now in the calm, timeless stillness of a sacred place, watching the white spires of pampas grass sway near the spot in the thicket where the deer had disappeared.

Arrow in the Neck

THERE WAS A RIGHT WAY and a wrong way to every-thing. From the time he was seven years old, Logan Fife had lived his life by this dictum, which had been drummed into his head by his father, Gerald Fife, Second Lieutenant, United States Marine Corps. And even though his father had been killed in Vietnam in March of 1967 when Logan was fourteen, he continued to live his life by the code of discipline his father had seared into his being through carpentry lessons, hunting and fishing trips, and summers of intense physical labor. Four more years of Catholic schooling only deepened the imprint.

When Logan married Jo Ann Bell two years out of high school and took a job as a trainee at the Northern Wyoming Smokejumper Center, he became even more focused and ex-act, more confirmed in his adherence to discipline. When his first two children, Jill and Melissa, came along, he molded them with fierce dedication to doing things the right way. No whining, no excuses, no escapism. He taught them well and with utmost respect and affection but never compromised for the sake of peace or in the face of tears. They became, as it was said at the Smoke Jumper's Center, troopers.

Once Logan Fife's son, Scott, joined the family, it appeared that this boy would be a crowning testimony to the ethics of his Marine Corps grandfather. Scott's grooming was intense, enthusiastic, and proud and was carried out without compro-mise for the first fourteen years of his life.

Scott was sixteen before he began to waver. He was kicked off the football team for missing too many practices. He was arrested for shoplifting a barbecued chicken from the rotisserie at Safeway. He was caught swimming naked with twin sister blondes in Sheridan's municipal pool at 2 a.m. These aberrations did not surface all at once; they arced across his last two years of high school and triggered severe reprisals and punishments from his father. Scott took the punishments in stride, exemplary in his contrition and in his amended behavior. Logan Fife, in spite of his anger, his embarrassment, and his disappointment, could see that this was not a bad boy, not an evil doer. The boy's mother had stood up for him also, and stood up to Logan in pointing out the bright side of her son's track record as a varsity wrestler, a community volunteer, and as a kid who cared about everyone from babies to the elderly.

Logan knew Jo Ann was right, but he had to fight furiously with the demons of his own standards to keep from savaging his son with harsh words and punishments. To have his son step out of line in what seemed such a cavalier fashion galled him to the quick. More than once he had to drive to the health club and play racquetball until he was ready to vomit before he could find the calm that loving his son called for. He found no solace in praying about the lapses in Scott's behavior. He preferred to chop wood instead, splitting the logs in perfect halves with an axe honed sharp as a guillotine. He had to draw an arrow to the maximum pull his bow would allow and see it pass through the chest of a deer, the fletching flickering as the arrow sailed into the dark border of trees at the edge of a meadow and the deer dropping to the ground like a box of rocks. Even that exactness was not always enough to set the scales in balance. Not until he had skinned and gutted and carved the deer into steaks and ground parts of it into long, even streaks of jerky, and fitted the wrapped steaks into the freezer in smooth, orderly stacks was he able to feel the anger lift.

For the first two years after Scott graduated high school, Logan Fife was given, as though a gift from the gods of temperance, a reprieve from any problems with Scott. The wheel of fortune seemed to be spinning in reverse. Scott got a part-time job at an REI store and enrolled in Northern Wyoming Community College. He began dating a girl from Rollins, who had aspirations of becoming an orthopedic surgeon, and he and Logan hunted deer and went trout fishing at every opportunity.

The second summer Scott was out of high school he spent time on a district fire crew, battling blazes in Wyoming and Montana and creating a reputation that was music to his father's ears. They never talked about Scott's pursuing a career as a smokejumper, but Logan Fife nurtured a secret hope that he didn't share even with the boy's mother. Though he was radical in his rejection of anything he considered pipe-dream nonsense, Logan had a streak of superstition he allowed some play in his character. There was always that little gadfly of perversity in life that you had to factor into your assumptions, like the impish musician in *Fiddler on the Roof.* He hated that little demon, but he knew better than to deny the fiddler's existence. So he let things ride and welcomed the uplifting steadiness he was seeing in his son.

Scott Fife got his first DUI a month after he turned twenty-one. His father's close friend, Cal Kroomquist, a lawyer who specialized in Wyoming DUI violations, kept Scott out of jail by challenging the reading of a breathalyzer test and by negotiating some community service for Scott. Logan considered taking Scott's car away from him, but Jo Ann talked him out of it, arguing that Scott needed the car to get to work and school. Stranding him that way just wasn't worth the risk. Logan agreed but still gave the boy a lengthy tongue-lashing.

For the next six months, Scott showed no signs of resentment toward his father. They went grouse hunting a couple times and to a gun show in Montana. Nothing was said about the DUI, although Logan stayed away from the country bars they sometimes visited on their outdoor trips. One night near Red Lodge, Montana, they met some loggers at a café, and the loggers talked them into joining them at the Hunting Lodge Bar across the street. Logan got excited by the camaraderie, drank more than he was used to drinking, and had to have Scott drive him back to camp. It was encouraging for Logan to see Scott drink only two beers in two hours and not be drawn into the reverie.

Logan was on a fire in Colorado when Scott got his second DUI.

● ● ●

Over a smoldering bed of campfire coals deep in the Big Horn Mountains, Logan listened while his son talked.

"It's not as bad as you think, Dad. That first one I was right on the line on the breathalyzer test. It could have gone either way. And the cop was clearly out to hammer me on the second one. You should have heard the way he talked to me."

Logan slid a spatula under the two trout he was frying. In the waning light, the shine of their skins and the red flicker of the slashes on their necks did not have the usual calming effect on him. "You're making excuses. A DUI is a DUI. And if you think Cal Kroomquist is going to get you off a third time, think again."

"But I wasn't being reckless on that second one. I had no idea the taillights were out on Blessinger's car. That's why we got stopped."

Logan slid the fish onto two plates next to a bed of fried potatoes.

"I've never had a ticket," he said. "Not even a parking ticket. You're a time bomb waiting to happen."

"Maybe you're luckier than I am, Dad. We're not the same person."

"Luck has nothing to do with it. It's choices, and you know it."

"OK, I made bad choices. But I'm not a criminal. I can change."

Logan looked at his son—the bright, intelligent eyes, the square jaw, and his mother's thick blonde hair. So much going for him and him jeopardizing it all. How did this happen?

"You can talk change," he said. "But your words don't hold water. We're going to have to try something else. You can't live at home any more. You need to be out on your own."

"I can't afford to do that. I'll have to quit school. How can you . . ."

"Because I have to. Because you're destroying my relationship with your mother, and with you."

"I don't see what this has to do with Mom."

"It has everything to do with her."

"Then let me stay. I can make things better. I'll stop partying."

"I'm giving you two weeks to find your own place."

Scott finished his meal and scraped the fish bones off his plate into the fire. They flared briefly, then shifted into the coals, their delicate tips glowing.

"I'll prove you wrong."

Logan didn't answer. He was staring at the dark wall of pines bordering the north edge of camp.

● ● ●

Eight months later, at two o'clock in the morning on a crisp, full-moon night in early October, Logan Fife was awakened by the harsh jingle of his landline by a call from the Sheridan County jail.

"Is this Logan?"

"Yes, it is. Who's this?"

"Jeff Redding."

"Jeff! What's up?"

"We have your son in custody here at the jail. Brought him in about forty minutes ago. Thought I'd best call you as soon as I could. The jail is really crowded tonight, so I'm checking to see if you want to come get him."

Redding paused.

"Course he could be back in here once he goes to court."

Logan sat up on the edge of the bed, could see the moon between the curtains, arresting in its luminosity.

"What's he in for, Jeff?"

"DUI. And leaving the scene of an accident. He didn't really go far; just wandered down the street from the taco truck he glanced off of. Sitting on the curb with his head in his hands when we got there."

"Is he OK?"

"He looks fine to me. He asked me not to call you. Said he'd be fine if he had to stay the night."

"Was anyone hurt?"

"Nope. The Mexicans who own the taco truck must have been sleeping in the park at the end of the block."

"Was Scott alone?"

"Far as we could tell."

"Damn it to hell, that's the . . ."

"What'd you say? Lot of noise down here."

In the brief hiatus before he spoke again, Logan Fife sensed a void opening in the night sky and the moon pulling back, dimming, shrinking, but when he looked again, it was still looming large, burning with a coppery glow. He knew the answer to the deputy's question before the question came.

"So do you want to come get your son, or do you want us to hold him over night?"

"I . . . I think he needs to stay there, Jeff; at least for tonight."

"We'll go ahead and put him in the communal cell then, if that's OK with you. The singles are all full, doubled up actually. Not sure what's gotten into people tonight."

Logan tried a half-hearted quip about the full moon. The deputy muttered something about werewolves; then said he had to get going, he had a bunch of people to book.

"You can come get him any time after eight in the morning. That's not far off."

"Not far," Logan said, but the figure of his sleeping wife on the far side of the bed seemed a galaxy away.

The telephone awakened him again at 4 a.m., and he was told when he answered it that he needed to come down to the jail right away. Jo Ann was wide awake this time and said she was going along, but Logan sensed he shouldn't let her. They argued intensely for a few minutes, but Jo Ann would not accept waiting for him to come back—she'd go in her own car if she had to. Logan told her to go ahead and get dressed but made her promise that she would stay in the courthouse lobby while he went up to the jail to check on Scott.

● ● ●

The seven-year-old Lakota boy feinted right, keeping his dribble, then cut left, circled behind Cody Birch, dribbled under the basket, glanced up at the bare hoop, dribbled back out to the far end of the cement pad, spun, dribbled past Cody in a burst of speed, looped behind the rusted pole holding the backboard and rim, dribbled straight at Cody, then stopped five feet away and stood bouncing the ball like he was tattooing Cody's face with it.

The Lakota boy had not known Cody long, did not expect him to charge. So he was totally surprised when the top of Cody's head speared into his chest, the ball flying off to his left, and then he was falling. He felt his shoulders hit the cement, but he somehow kept his head from snapping back, relieved, but only for a few seconds, because closed-fist blows were peppering his neck and face. He managed to cross his forearms over his face and ward off most of the blows while yelling, "Get off! Get off!" But the blows kept coming, some of them pounding him in the chest and stomach, and one connecting with his nose, which started to bleed, and he thought he was going to pass out.

Suddenly, he felt the other boy's body lifting off him, and he hovered in the terrifying lull, waiting to see the ratty red cowboy boots moving away on the cement. This did not occur. Instead, when he rolled over to get up, the first kick caught him in the ribs. Then another sent a fiery pain through his knee and another into his lower back. Then the kicks were coming from every direction, and the Lakota boy couldn't tell which way to dodge the flurry of ferocious kicks. They seemed endless, and when they got closer to his shoulders and head, he began to scream.

That was when the elderly Lakota woman burst out the door of a nearby trailer house, tossing her shawl aside as she hurried down the wooden steps of the porch. She was across the yard and behind Cody Birch, her long fingers locking on the collar of his shirt as he was drawing his leg back. She dragged Birch, off-balance, across the grass between two trailers until she reached a sandbox made from railroad ties, and flung him into it. Then she hurried over to help her grandson stand up, guiding him over to her trailer, glancing one time with the glare of a hawk at Cody Birch before she quickly ushered her grandson inside and slammed the door.

Cody Birch lay in the hot, dirty sand which smelled of creosote and cat shit, sand caked at the corners of his eyes and his mouth full of sand. These were the taste and texture of his life—the bitter, dry grit of his mornings, afternoons and nights; the coarse, nasty granules of time falling into the ever widening wound of his isolation. He sat up, peering down the street at the skyline of Box Elder, South Dakota, a combination prairie town and rural slum strung across the clay and alkali flats only a few miles east of Rapid City. It was a 1980s version of Steinbeck's Hooverville, and in July it seemed to writhe and wither in the sun and scorching wind, its inhabitants eking out an existence amidst the trailer parks and shanties, the abandoned tractors and tumbledown garages and sheds, the stripped and rusting trucks, the crumbling, oxidized vans and cars, windshields shattered, pack rats ripping the remaining stuffing from seats. It was a place for the dispossessed descendants of the old gold seekers, the railroad builders, the hard-bitten cowhands and homesteaders, a boiling pot for drifters and oil field workers, and broken-bodied truckers and welders and mechanics. It had a few stores and bars and an elementary school, and it clung to the soil like the bitter blue sage that filled its yards.

This is where Cody Birch was born and had lived with his mother, an exotic dancer at the Buffalo Bill Bar in Rapid City, and her ever-changing string of boyfriends. Some of them ignored Cody totally, some taught him to curse and bare-knuckle box, some answered his little boy antics with back-handed slaps and kicks in the ribs. This is where Cody Birch went to first grade and couldn't keep up with the other kids, couldn't comprehend the alphabet, had no books at home, no crayons or pencils, no covers on his bed except for a U-Haul blanket, no toys but the grasshoppers and spiders he kept in jars he dug from the foul smelling soil at the junkyard just south of Bitter Creek. This is where he was shunned by other children, who had nothing also but did have soap and a few clothes at home so that they felt justified in telling him that he smelled like a cow pie and that he was dumb and ugly and belonged in a pig pen.

He was neither dumb nor ugly, but he knew of no way to ward off abuse except with his hands and feet. So he became a fighter, a fierce and merciless attack dog his hecklers came to fear and eventually leave alone. But by then he had become inseparable from his own violence, and his rage only grew with his body so that, at eleven, he had the temperament of a wounded bear. His explosiveness caught his adversaries off guard, and before they knew what had happened, they were on the ground with blows raining down on them in the form of Cody Birch's fists or in the savage staccato of his booted feet.

Birch's barely contained rage followed him through middle school in Gillette, Wyoming, and to tenth grade in Cheyenne, where he quit school at sixteen and, after lying about his age, went to work at a bentonite plant north of Belle Fourche, South Dakota. For the next ten years he was a rolling stone, who punched and bit and kicked more people than he could remember and who got thrown into jail after jail until he finally changed weapons, stabbed a deputy sheriff in Thermopolis, and ended up in the state penitentiary. But for once in his life the stars lined up in his favor; the deputy pulled through surgery and lived so that Birch's sentence got shortened, and he was eventually paroled. He drifted north and took a job mending fences on a farm east of Sheridan, Wyoming, just six months from the night he crossed paths with Scott Fife in the Sheridan County jail.

● ● ●

Logan Fife almost didn't recognize his son when he entered the cell and saw the prone figure lying on a cot in the center of the room. The lumpy face and puffed-shut eyes, blood co-agulating at the corners, the lips swollen to twice their normal size, the flattened bridge of the nose, the blotchy purple cast to the face, and the bloat of the neck made Scott barely recogniz-able. In fact, Logan's mind took a sudden detour into thinking it wasn't Scott.

When he came closer to the cot, the recognition stabbed him in the brain and squeezed his heart to a frozen walnut in his chest. His throat seized with a sudden ache deeper than any choke-up he'd ever felt, and he was suddenly on his knees beside the cot, one hand clamped on the boy's bruised fore-arm, as though to make the profoundly still body more real. A low, wailing moan rose in his chest and gained volume by the time it poured uncontrollably from his mouth. The law officers gathered in the booking room down the hall heard the sound through the hollow doors and the thinly plastered walls as it grew in resonance and pitch. They did not look at one another but fastened their eyes on oddly irrelevant objects— the Royal Crown calendar on the wall, their key rings, dead hornets on the windowsills, a pearl-handled letter opener on the desk—while the sound of Logan's voice filled their ears.

Somewhere in the visceral rush of his agony, Logan, glancing at the senseless graffiti on the far wall, cried out to everyone and no one, "Who did this to my boy? Who did this to my boy?"

When he was given the answer by the sheriff in an interrogation room twenty minutes later, he leaped from his chair, surging toward the door, and had to be wrestled to the floor by the sheriff and two deputies, all the while yelling, "I'll kill the bastard. I'll kill him!"

Only Jo Ann's voice coaxing him back to earth once she had been summoned to the jail from the courthouse lobby was able to silence him, to hold him in a nearly catatonic trance, so that the officers could help him up and sit him in a chair. Deputy Jeff Redding, wanting to help Logan understand what had happened, was able to get Logan's attention long enough to explain that, according to some prisoners who had witnessed the fight, Scott Fife had been minding his own business at the end of a bench in the rear of the communal cell when he happened to look up and catch the eye of a thirty-two-year-old drifter on the other side of the room. The drifter, a man named Cody Birch, already high on the drugs he had been trying to sell at a truck stop north of town, had been needling other prisoners for several hours, muttering about kicking someone's ass, but got no takers to respond to his insults. So when Scott Fife caught his eye, Birch fixed on Scott immediately, leering across the cell as he spat out, "What're you lookin' at?" And Scott, still feeling his own liquor, had made the mistake of tossing out a comeback with, "I'm not sure what I'm lookin' at," and looked away.

From that point on, the witness said, it was only a matter of time before Cody Birch fidgeted his way to the other end of the cell, and only a matter of seconds before he had grabbed the front of Scott's shirt and pulled him out to the center of the room. As one witness put it, it was like when you break a rack of billiard balls. Everyone cleared to the edges of the room while the older man stood glaring at the younger one, the majority of them following an unspoken jailhouse code.

Even after the scuffle began, only a few still looked on. Even after Scott, with what looked to be the skill of a trained wrestler, managed to get Birch in a headlock, and Birch had started growling and cursing, only the few took furtive glances. And when Birch broke Scott's grip with a fierce blow to the stomach, which doubled Scott up on the floor, only one old man, too drunk and too weary to care what Birch might do to him later, looked on. It was he who told Jeff Redding about the worst beating he'd ever seen, about the kicking he thought would never end, how he thought at least some of the others would come forward and stop the madness, how two muscular bikers didn't intervene until it was too late. Once they pulled Birch away, the old man added, Birch had turned and walked over to a chair he'd been sitting on earlier and which remained empty, and sat down and studied his boots as though he were stewing about the bloodstains on the toes.

Logan Fife's urge to kill Cody Birch came flooding back, and his mind darted this way and that, seeking a way he might gain access to the room where Birch was being held. But the sound of Jo Ann's voice drew him away from any thoughts of Cody Birch, and now it was his turn to hear his wife's voice alternating between screams and sobs as she lay across her son's body and cried, "No, no, no . . ."

Logan snapped out of his trance then and convinced the officers to let him go to her. He lifted her away from the body and held her more closely than he'd ever held her—an embrace of one flesh, as in the one flesh they'd become in giving life to the silent boy lying on the cot. There was no speaking—no accusations, no rebukes, no pledges or resolutions. They could only stand there, so locked in the core of the present that the future collapsed and went black.

● ● ●

For three years following Scott's death, Logan tried all kinds of ways to reclaim his old place in the scheme of things and to feel something other than pain. He bore down on novice fire crews even beyond the grueling, two-week hiking ordeals he usually put them through. He jumped into fires with abandon and fought flames long after the rest of the crew had crawled exhausted into their tents. He hunted alone, tracking deer and elk with inordinate cunning. He ran naked through the forest and drank deer blood. He kayaked down Montana's Yellowstone River with almost supernatural grace, knifed through every dangerous drop and boulder-strewn passage. He dared the river to kill him, outfoxing it at every turn.

His gambits seemed to bounce off the emptiness of it all. This infuriated him but only briefly; then the flame flicked out, and the ache returned.

● ● ●

Jo Ann Fife could hold it against him forever, re-play that night again and again on the memory reel, hate him and his hard-nosed beliefs, blame him for the loss of her son with boundless rage and overwhelming bitterness. She could touch and be touched and feel nothing at all, just distance without dimension, a stillness in motion. She could have the utmost compassion for him, see in his eyes and hear in his voice the price he had paid attempting to do what he thought was right and necessary, only to have it all explode in his face. She could pray for strength of heart and peace of mind, the will to go on, to get up in the morning. She could focus on her daughters, her beautiful, vibrant daughters, and heal herself in loving them at a new level of gratitude and hope. She could bury herself in work, in caring for and encouraging home-less women, in learning from them that she was not alone in her suffering. She could borrow their courage and their deep inner beauty and grow a new heart. She could cling to her son in her thought and memory, and in every detail and image that brought him back to her, if only for a minute, an hour. She could smell him in a tee-shirt crumpled on a closet floor, see him sitting in the empty lifeguard chair at the city pool. She could feel the prickles of his crazy spike haircut in a cheesy second-grade photo. She could let go of all railings against God and fate, against the blood-stained horror of it all. She could seek beauty and goodness and laughter and good will and generosity; she could feed on positive things, on the energy of life.

She was driving out of Bridgewater, South Dakota, after a week-long visit with her aging mother, watching the prairie open into the unending distances of her home state. Ten miles east of Michell she began to pass large fields of sunflowers flar-ing from the edges of the freeway into the far reaches of the horizon. They stretched in waves of black faces rimmed with bright yellow petals, their fully-bloomed heads tilted toward the rising sun. They were all on the south side of the freeway, rolling back, back in an almost hypnotic sweep. Jo Ann was so drawn to the dazzling maze of their symmetry that she took the first exit she saw for a frontage road, made her way across the overpass, and drove down the old highway until she could park at the edge of a field.

The morning air was still cool even though it was August. It cooled even more as she walked along the shadowed dirt path between two enormous stands of flowers, their wide, vibrant faces turning in unison far above her head. The path seemed to bore forever into the tangled stalks, and she walked until she spotted an opening where she could enter the field to her right. There was enough space between the rows that she could lose herself in the jungle of stalks, glancing up intermittently at the concentric circles, the rings of florets darkening from gold to maroon to the black star pupil in the center of each face. They hung in the sky like a constellation of ancient masks, floating, lighting every crevice of her mind, unburdening her heart through their blazing alliance with the sun.

● ● ●

It was the perfect shot, or what seemed like the perfect shot—the elk stone still on a knoll at the center of the shooting lane, its antlers framed, as in a painting, by a border of evening shadows and set against a sun-guttering meadow that flowed back, back into a wall of dark trees.

Logan Fife had nocked the arrow with intense concentration and stealth, gauging the forty-yard shot with machine-like precision. The elk filled the moment and the space it occupied with timeless poise and alertness as it stared down the ravine from which it expected the challenger to emerge, unaware that the bugling it had identified as a rival bull's claim to its harem had been sounded by Logan Fife.

The stage Logan had been dreaming of for almost six years was set. He had dropped a large bull with a long distance shot during rifle season five years earlier, and the thrill of he and Scott tracking it down and carrying it out of the woods resonated in his memory. But this was even better. This elk was equal in size and had a rack of antlers that looked sure to break a state record.

To Logan's great surprise, the arrow, at first lifting almost imperceptibly, rose significantly by the time it reached the elk, which, suddenly spooked, had lurched at such an angle that the arrow pierced the thick fur of its neck. With the arrow protruding from both sides of its neck, the elk darted away as though nothing had happened.

Logan was stunned, his legs locked, as he stared at the empty shooting lane, then into the trees that had swallowed the elk. He came to his senses quickly, brushed off the demons already hounding him about a bad shot, knowing he had to track the elk down right away. But as he ran along the edge of the meadow, worry began to dog him. Surely the elk would bleed to death and drop to the ground shortly. Or it would try to hide, and he'd follow the trail of blood until he could catch up and put the elk out of its misery.

As he made his way through brambles and bushes, wound around tree trunks, leaping over rocks, the bow jouncing wildly and the arrows clacking in their quiver, he still could not believe that his shot had gone wrong. He had taken such a solid bead, the bow and arrow feeling a part of his body with a fullness and clarity from which everything else—past, present, and future—fell away. Yet the shot had gone awry, and the elk had transformed into something freakish, turning everything upside down.

He was starting to panic when he noticed blood spots on some leaves, then some drops on a boulder blocking the trail. He gathered his wits, called up his most reliable woodsman's skills, and trusted his reading of signs. The signs came fewer and farther between, and the light, splintered by the trunks of pines, began to wane. If he didn't find the elk soon, he'd have to return tomorrow, or the next day, or the day after that. And search and search and comb every inch of ground and backtrack and circle and leave markers.

Logan saw now from the darkening of the trees that he would be lost in the woods shortly if he didn't return to his camp. He stopped at the edge of a ravine, eyes still sifting the slopes between trees, the openings between bushes, the distant beds of pine needles. He took out a handkerchief and tied it on a branch stub at a place he'd last seen blood, and he cut notches in a couple of fire-scarred trees as he made his way up the mountainside.

At dawn Logan returned to the spot he had shot the elk and worked deeper into the forest between two steep mountains, but found no sign of the elk, so he broke camp and went home. Two days later he drove back into the mountains but went beyond the turn-off to his original campsite and entered heavier timber. For the next four hours he hiked through nearly impenetrable undergrowth, waded streams, and climbed rock slides until his fingers were bleeding.

By late afternoon Logan was approaching delirium and was seeing the elk with the arrow in its neck feinting at him and dodging behind trees. He slowed his pace and eased the churning of his mind. It came to him that he had unaccountably spaced off his own recollections of stories he'd heard from other hunters about seeing deer and elk running through the woods with arrows protruding from shoulders and rib cages. And stories he'd been told about people finding, while dressing out deer, arrowheads or bullet slugs embedded in crusted over pockets of flesh and hide. The chances were equally good, then, that the elk might still be alive and would survive the wound. It might already have rejoined its harem and was leading them to higher ground, the ends of the arrow glancing off branches or snagging on leaves, only to tear loose and go wherever the elk went. Or the arrow had broken off on one or both sides, and the elk was then able to maneuver as before, stronger in some bizarre way for taking the arrow into itself, into its wildness, and struggling on. In the end, Logan knew now that he had to stop searching and let the elk go. It was OK to let it go; there was nothing more he could do.

He cut through a patch of clover and sat down on the stump of a tree that had been toppled by lightning. The forest in front of him seemed a leering maze of color and shadow. With its intricately woven veneer, it hid everything that needed hiding; it had reclaimed the elk with brute defiance. There was no way to right what had happened to the elk. It wasn't even a matter of right and wrong. It just happened in hunting, and he couldn't change it any more than he could change what had happened to Scott. He simply could not control the movement of the world. He was in the world, whether or not he wanted to be in it, but he was not in charge of it; he could not unswervingly make it conform to his demands. He realized then that he would never be at peace with what had happened to his son, yet taking total responsibility for it was inaccurate and unhealthy. Blame and shame were killing him, and he wanted, in the worst way, to live.

Tugging his cap in place and adjusting the straps on his backpack, Logan rose from the stump and looked at a stand of trees near the rim of the ravine he would follow in returning to his truck. He didn't see the woodpecker at first, but then caught sight of it flying from one tree to another, securing its hold on the trunk with tiny claws, testing the bark with its power drill beak, seeking a feast in the primal resistance of wood.

acknowledgments

Grateful acknowledgment is made to the following publications in which several of these stories first appeared.

Blueline: "When the Buffalo Roam"

The Briar Cliff Review: "Bottom Dweller," "The Recovering Dairy Farmer"

The Chariton Review: Winter of the Great White Wolf: "The Saga of Webster World Turner," "Appendix to the Air King Cell Phone Owner's Manual"

North American Review: "Girl on a Float," "Arrow in the Neck," "Curse of the Corn Borer," "The Fallen"

Paddlefish: "Big House on the Prairie"

Rosebud: "Crop Duster"

South Dakota Magazine: "Stingray"

Sudden Fiction Youth: "Coyote Bait"

about the author

Brian Bedard is Emeritus Professor of English at the University of South Dakota, where he directed the creative writing program and also served as Editor of *The South Dakota Review* from 1995 to 2011. His short stories have appeared widely in such forums as *Quarterly West, North American Review, Alaska Quarterly Review, Cimarron Review,* and *North Dakota Quarterly.* His first collection of stories, *Hour of the Beast and Other Stories,* was published by Chariton Review Press. His second collection of stories, *Grieving on the Run,* won the Serena McDonald Kennedy Award from Snake Nation Press, and was published by Snake Nation Press in 2007 and nominated by that press for the National Book Award in 2008. The South Dakota Council of Teachers of English honored Brian as the 2008 South Dakota Author of the Year. At present he lives with his wife, Sharon, in Spokane, Washington, where he is a member of the English Department at Gonzaga University.

about the press

North Dakota State University Press (NDSU Press) exists to stimulate and coordinate interdisciplinary regional scholarship. These regions include the Red River Valley, the state of North Dakota, the plains of North America (comprising both the Great Plains of the United States and the prairies of Canada), and comparable regions of other continents. We publish peer reviewed regional scholarship shaped by national and international events and comparative studies.

Neither topic nor discipline limits the scope of NDSU Press publications. We consider manuscripts in any field of learning. We define our scope, however, by a regional focus in accord with the press's mission. Generally, works published by NDSU Press address regional life directly, as the subject of study. Such works contribute to scholarly knowledge of region (that is, discovery of new knowledge) or to public consciousness of region (that is, dissemination of information, or interpretation of regional experience). Where regions abroad are treated, either for comparison or because of ties to those North American regions of primary concern to the press, the linkages are made plain. For nearly three-quarters of a century, NDSU Press has published substantial trade books, but the line of publications is not limited to that genre. We also publish textbooks (at any level), reference books, anthologies, reprints, papers, proceedings, and monographs. The press also considers works of poetry or fiction, provided they are established regional classics or they promise to assume landmark or reference status for the region. We select biographical or autobiographical works carefully for their prospective contribution to regional knowledge and culture. All publications, in whatever genre, are of such quality and substance as to embellish the imprint of NDSU Press.

We changed our imprint to North Dakota State University Press in January 2016. Prior to that, and since 1950, we published as the North Dakota Institute for Regional Studies Press. We continue to operate under the umbrella of the North Dakota Institute for Regional Studies, located at North Dakota State University.